IMPERIAL SPLENDOUR

Barbara Cartland

Barbara Cartland Ebooks Ltd

This edition © 2020

Copyright Cartland Promotions 1979

ISBNs

9781788672856   EPUB

9781788672863   PAPERBACK

Book design by M-Y Books
m-ybooks.co.uk

THE BARBARA CARTLAND
ETERNAL COLLECTION

The Barbara Cartland Eternal Collection is the unique opportunity to collect all five hundred of the timeless beautiful romantic novels written by the world's most celebrated and enduring romantic author.

Named the Eternal Collection because Barbara's inspiring stories of pure love, just the same as love itself, the books will be published on the internet at the rate of four titles per month until all five hundred are available.

The Eternal Collection, classic pure romance available worldwide for all time .

THE LATE DAME BARBARA CARTLAND

Barbara Cartland, who sadly died in May 2000 at the grand age of ninety eight, remains one of the world's most famous romantic novelists. With worldwide sales of over one billion, her outstanding 723 books have been translated into thirty six different languages, to be enjoyed by readers of romance globally.

Writing her first book 'Jigsaw' at the age of 21, Barbara became an immediate bestseller. Building upon this initial success, she wrote continuously throughout her life, producing bestsellers for an astonishing 76 years. In addition to Barbara Cartland's legion of fans in the UK and across Europe, her books have always been immensely popular in the USA. In 1976 she achieved the unprecedented feat of having books at numbers 1 & 2 in the prestigious B. Dalton Bookseller bestsellers list.

Although she is often referred to as the 'Queen of Romance', Barbara Cartland also wrote several historical biographies, six autobiographies and numerous theatrical plays as well as books on life, love, health and cookery. Becoming one of Britain's most popular media personalities and dressed in her trademark pink, Barbara spoke on radio and television about social and political issues, as well as making many public appearances.

In 1991 she became a Dame of the Order of the British Empire for her contribution to literature and her work for humanitarian and charitable causes.

Known for her glamour, style, and vitality Barbara Cartland became a legend in her own lifetime. Best remembered for her wonderful romantic novels and loved by millions of readers worldwide, her books remain treasured for their heroic heroes, plucky heroines and traditional values. But above all, it was Barbara Cartland's overriding belief in the positive power of love to help, heal and improve the quality of life for everyone that made her truly unique.

AUTHOR'S NOTE

As Napoleon waited impatiently in Moscow for an Armistice, the vacillating Russian Czar Alexander was transformed into a man fortified by deep religious fervour. He replied that he would not negotiate while 'one enemy soldier remains on Russian soil'.

After five weeks Napoleon had no option but to withdraw his Army and begin the long trek home. But he had left it too late.

On November 4th the snow began to fall and two days later the temperature was many degrees below freezing. Lack of food and clothing and the savagery of the Russian peasants resulted in the roads being strewn with dead men, guns and horses. Half a million of the *Grande Armée* failed to reach France.

In April 1813 Napoleon abdicated and was exiled to the island of Elba. When Alexander entered Paris the crowds went wild and his own country begged him to accept the title of 'Alexander the Blessed'. It was the Czar who, at the conquest of Vienna, first had the idea of a League of Nations.

The Russians rebuilt Moscow and, when I visited Leningrad, now St. Petersburg, in 1978 I could see how brilliantly they had rebuilt that City after the terrible devastation left by the Germans in 1941. The Palaces that had been looted, shelled and blown up by mines are now elaborate, splendid and exactly as when they were designed on the order of Catherine the Great.

The famous Duke of Wellington in 1826 thought St. Petersburg 'the most beautiful City on earth'.

Armand-Emmanuel Due de Richelieu (1766-1822) held the post of Governor-General of New Russia until 1815. After the War he was twice Prime Minister of France under King Louis XVIII.

Les Sylphides launched the whole Romantic period of the ballet and was performed in Paris in March 1832, in London in July and in St. Petersburg in September.

The costume attributed to Eugène Lami with the long bell-shaped skirt, became the accepted attire of ballerinas of the period and is still worn. Because it is so familiar, and I wanted my readers to know exactly how Zoia looked, I have anticipated its first performance in St. Petersburg by twenty years.

This book is dedicated to a good friend of mine, The Earl Mountbatten of Burma, who first suggested that I should visit Russia to obtain the background for a novel. He also helped me with many authentic details of the period.

CHAPTER ONE
1812

The Duke of Welminster walked across the room to pull back the curtains from the window and stare out at the Neva.

In the pale sunlight, which later would deepen to a red heat, the river, one of the shortest in the world, was shimmering on the water.

It reflected the bright and shining gold on the needle-like spire on the Peter and Paul Cathedral on the far shore and the Duke could also see the bastions and battlements of the Fortress built by Peter the Great.

He was for the moment, however, not concerned with the beauty of St. Petersburg, which had left him somewhat surprised by the perfection of its architecture, but with the Russian Army awaiting their Commanders-in-Chief's conclusion as to the direction that the French intended to advance.

The Duke's contemplation was interrupted by a soft cry of protest.

"Have you forgotten me?" a woman's voice asked. "I am still here and wanting you."

There was no mistaking the invitation and the seductive undertone that made the words, spoken in English but with a distinct trace of a Russian accent, sound passionately alluring.

The Duke turned round with a smile on his lips.

There was no doubt that the Princess Katharina Bagration was very lovely, in fact one of the loveliest women that he had ever seen.

Lying back against the lace-edged pillows with her hair falling over her white shoulders and her huge eyes seeming to fill her whole face, she looked very much younger than she actually was.

There was a distinct Oriental mystery about her, an Andalusian charm and, when she was dressed, a Parisian elegance.

It was not surprising, the Duke thought, that the Czar Alexander I had chosen her to spy on him, a fact that he had been aware of from the moment he had arrived in the City of St. Petersburg.

The Duke was very experienced in the art of intrigue and had carried out a number of unofficial Diplomatic missions with such success that he had not been surprised when the Prime Minister, Lord Liverpool, had sent for him.

"I want your help, Welminster," he began, "and I think you can guess where I wish you to go."

"To Russia?" the Duke had queried.

"Exactly," the Prime Minister replied.

Lord Castlereagh, the Foreign Secretary, who was in the Cabinet Room, interposed to add,

"For God's sake, Welminster, please find out what is happening. The reports I receive contradict themselves to the point where I don't know whether I am on my head or my heels as far as that enigmatic country is concerned."

The irritation in the Foreign Secretary's voice was very evident and the Duke could well understand his frustration.

Czar Alexander had kept not just the British but most of Europe seriously confused by his behaviour during the last few years.

And even Napoleon Bonaparte might be excused for finding him incomprehensible.

Having moved through the first years of his reign at the beginning of the century, as a shadowy indecisive figure, Alexander's attention had become focused on Bonaparte.

The Corsican's astonishing Military successes had turned the whole of Europe into a turmoil.

The Czar could not make up his mind whether to join a coalition against the French or to try to continue his father's policy of friendship.

Napoleon had actually suggested to Czar Paul, his father, that France and Russia should partition the world, but, when Bonaparte had trampled into the dust the terms of the Treaty of Amiens, the Russian Sovereign had written that he seemed to be 'one of the most infamous tyrants that history has ever produced'.

After the great disaster at the Battle of Austerlitz, when the twenty-eight year old Czar Alexander, leading his Army as its Commander-in-Chief, had been completely routed, his gallantry had seemed to desert him.

He had ridden away from the battlefield alone, dismounted and collapsed under an apple tree, where he had wept convulsively.

Although he tried to excuse himself by blaming the Austrians, the Russians suffered yet another disastrous defeat at the Battle of Friedland.

It was then, to the amazement of the Russian people, that Alexander had signed 'a Treaty of Friendship' with the French when he had promised faithfully that he would take part in the Continental Blockade of trade against England.

This had brought him extreme unpopularity with the Russian people together with the fact that they could not adjust themselves after Catherine the Great's victories to a number of ignominious defeats.

In the previous year, 1811, Alexander had listened to his subjects and refused to send soldiers to fight for the French and, what was more, he had refused to close Russian Ports to neutral shipping and uphold the Blockade against England.

"I cannot help thinking," a famous British General had said to the Duke in London, "that if it comes to a showdown, Russia will prove a poor match for Napoleon's Grand Army."

The Duke had felt inclined to agree with him, but now that he was actually in Russia he began to have his doubts.

Indeed yesterday the Czar had shown him a letter from Count Rostopchin, the Governor of Moscow, he had found the contents very convincing.

The Governor had written,

"Your Empire, Sire, has two powerful defenders, its vast space and its climate. The Emperor of all Russia will be formidable at Moscow, terrible at Karzan and invincible at Tobolsk."

"Stop thinking about war, Blake," the Princess Katharina now cried insistently. "I can find something far more interesting to talk about."

The Duke standing by the bed, knew what such a conversation involved, but instead of surrendering to the invitation of her lips he replied,

"I think it is time you returned to your own room."

"There is no hurry."

"I am thinking of your reputation."

The Princess laughed and it was a low musical sound.

"You are the only man I know who is so considerate or is it perhaps that I am boring you?"

There was no doubt she assumed that was an impossibility and the Duke, with just a touch of cynicism in his voice, answered,

"How could I be so ungallant?"

"You are very handsome, *mon cher*," the Princess pouted, "as far too many women have told you. I adore handsome men and no man could be a more alluring lover."

She had then broken into French, as if it was easier to express herself in that language when she spoke of love.

French was the language of the Nobility in St. Petersburg and French culture was a status symbol.

Someone had told the Duke on his arrival,

"Everything is uneatable for dinner if it is not first dressed by a French chef, no gown is elegant if it is not a Parisian one and yet there is surely no one in the whole City who does not blaspheme against Bonaparte and lament Lord Nelson!"

"You are very beautiful, Katharina," the Duke said now in French," but I still think that you should leave me for what is left of the night."

The Princess made a petulant little sound. Then, bending forward to reveal the exquisite curves of her naked breasts, she put her hand on the Duke's.

"You are too serious," she murmured, "let's be happy and enjoy ourselves. After all what is Russia to you?"

"An ally," the Duke replied, "if a somewhat vacillating one."

Katharina laughed softly and then she asked,

"Tell me what you want to know about your 'ally' and I will give you the right answers."

"I am sure of that," he replied. "I am only wondering what such information will cost me."

Katharina laughed again.

She was well aware that the Duke knew why she had sought him out, why she had flirted enticingly with him since he had arrived at The Winter Palace and why last night after he had retired to bed a secret panel in the wall of his bedroom had opened suddenly and then she had appeared unexpectedly.

That was not entirely true, because the Duke had been expecting her, although not in the particular manner by which she had affected her entrance.

"You know, of course," Lord Castlereagh had said to him in London, "that the Czar employs some of the loveliest women in St. Petersburg to spy on our Ambassador and any other Emissary we may send to Russia."

He had seen the smile on the Duke's face and added,

"Not that, Welminster, it will be a novelty for you."

"I will admit that it has happened in the past," the Duke replied, "and, having heard of the beauty of the women at the Court of St. Petersburg, I am quite looking forward to the experience."

"Be careful," the Foreign Secretary warned him.

"Of what?" the Duke enquired. "Giving away State secrets, most of which I suspect are known to the Russians already, or of losing my heart?"

"The latter has not entered into my calculations," Lord Castlereagh replied with a touch of irony.

The Duke had been expecting an enchantress, but he had to give the Czar full marks for his choice of the Princess.

As it happened, the Duke already knew a great deal about Katharina Bagration. She was half-Russian, half-Polish and had married at twenty a General many years older than herself.

A Countess in her own right with Royal blood in her veins, she was, with her husband, admitted to the highest circles of the Russian Court.

The fact that she was highly intelligent as well as beautiful, together with the traces in her of a Mongolian ancestry, gave her the faint air of Oriental mystery that made her unique even amongst a host of other beautiful Russian women.

It was the Czar who had ordered his Foreign Minister to use this effervescent and lovely young woman as a spy.

The Duke had already heard what had happened at Katharina's first assignment.

She had been told to make the acquaintance of Count Metternich, the Austrian delegate to Dresden, who the Russian Diplomats in Vienna insisted was of far greater importance than his youth and minor appointment suggested.

Count Metternich, then an almost unknown young man, was described on the secret files in the Kremlin as an intimate of the Emperor of Austria and the instrument who had been primarily responsible for the downfall of Thugut.

Princess Katharina, young, lovely, but with a shrewd little mind well hidden behind her childlike face, had called at the Legation in Dresden and, as a footman opened the door, it happened that Count Metternich was passing through the hall.

He was expecting the arrival of one of the Imperial Couriers with grave news.

Then framed in the sunlight against the dark hallway he saw a small exquisite figure.

She was wearing one of the thin, almost transparent muslin gowns that were the fashion and against the sun her body showed through the diaphanous material like a beautiful marble statue.

Count Metternich was for the moment spellbound into a strange stillness.

He said afterwards to one of his friends who repeated it to the Duke,

"She was like a beautiful naked angel."

At that moment the young Austrian and the Russian Secret Agent fell in love.

Their affair was a wild, fiery and insatiable union of all-consuming passion that had all Dresden talking.

The Duke had trained himself to file away information about people, especially those concerned in the Diplomatic world and he remembered as soon as he was introduced to Princess Katharina in The Winter Palace that he had been told that within three months of her meeting with Count Metternich, she found that she was to have a child.

This had been whispered about, argued over, discussed and re-discussed and there was actually a great deal of speculation as to what would happen next.

In fact, the Duke recalled, there had been an urgent command from the Czar, who wished to safeguard his beautiful agent's reputation at all costs.

General Bagration went through the ritual of announcing that his marriage was shortly to be blessed with a child and after the birth of a daughter he formally acknowledged paternity.

The Czar was no less accommodating and the Court of St. Petersburg formally recorded the birth.

The baby was summarily handed over to Count Metternich's adoring, patient and very understanding wife.

Utterly without conscience about the love-children he fathered, he was only grateful that his love affair could continue and, whatever was said privately, there would be no outward scandal.

Ten years later the Duke, however, was quite certain that, because Katharina had been so successful with by now the most outstanding Diplomat in Europe, the Czar had chosen her to win another triumph where he himself was concerned.

He was certain that the efficiency of the Russian Secret Service had noted that he was most fastidious where women were concerned, that he was the most sought-after bachelor in England and that, if they had recorded his many love affairs, they would doubtless by this time have filled many files in the Diplomatic archives.

At the same time he found Katharine's expertise and her sophisticated art in love-making a very pleasant part of his visit.

The Duke was, however, quite ruthless where his own interests were concerned.

If he had been approached by a woman who did not attract him or by one who offended his very fastidious taste when making love, he would have had no compunction about locking his door or, if that had proved ineffective, of turning her out of his bed.

But Katharina had appealed to him sensually and her body was, as many other men had found, irresistible.

The Duke had thought, as the passion they felt for each other burst into flame in the huge carved and gilded bed in a room decorated in the French manner and filled with priceless pictures that Catherine the Great's agents had bought in France, that she was the complement to everything that proclaimed culture.

When she had captured Count Metternich's heart, she had been very young and perhaps he had been her first lover after her marriage.

But now, the Duke thought, she had blossomed into a woman polished like a flawless gem into a brilliance that aroused the endless admiration of the mind as well as the desires of the body.

The Duke enjoyed the duels that they exchanged with words, both witty and provocative, even while she used every feminine wile to enslave him physically.

Now, as he looked at her with his grey eyes, she leaned back against the pillows and with her long-fingered little hands pulled the sheet over her nakedness until it was just beneath her chin.

There was something young and modest in the movement and yet at the same time it was a deliberately seductive action thought out and perhaps practised like the ritual steps of a ballerina. And the Duke appreciated the very artistry of it.

"What do you think about, Katharina," he asked, "when you are not 'working'?"

For a moment she looked at him doubtfully and then made no pretence not to understand the innuendo that lay behind his words.

"Now I am thinking of you," she said softly, "and there is no reason to think of myself."

It was an answer, he reflected that revealed the very subtlety of her mind.

Who else would she think about when she was not acting on the Czar's instructions, but about herself, her fiery, passionate Russian nature making it an absorbing subject?

The Duke glanced towards the elaborate gold and diamond encrusted clock that stood on the marble mantelpiece.

It was one of hundreds of beautiful clocks that decorated the glorious apartments of The Winter Palace, which on three floors extended for half a mile and had been part of Peter the Great's supreme collection.

"It is five o'clock," he observed, "and in four hours I have promised to breakfast with the Czar. Until then I intend to sleep, Katharina."

There was a note in his voice that told her it would be useless to plead with him.

She merely smiled and, rising from the bed apparently completely unselfconscious of her nakedness, she walked to a chair where she had thrown down the elaborate satin and lace *negligée* which she had entered the room in.

She might have had a child, but her body was still that of the beautiful naked angel as Clement Metternich had described her.

Wrapped in her *negligée*, she slipped her feet into a pair of velvet mules embroidered with pearls.

"Sleep well, my adorable Englishman," she purred. "I shall count the hours until I can kiss you again."

She flashed him a smile that gave her face a sudden witchery and she then moved across the room.

She touched the panel in the wall. It opened and, without looking back, she stepped into the dark aperture. Then the panelling swung back and closed behind her.

The Duke sat still for a moment and then he climbed into bed and closed his eyes, but he found, however, that the sleep he desired eluded him for the moment.

His brain was still active and again he was thinking not of Katharina and the fire that they had ignited in each other, but of Russia and the *Grand Armée* of France. Six hundred thousand men strong and immensely impressive.

Equally the Duke argued with himself that a third of the soldiers were unwilling German conscripts drawn from subject territories.

The first thing he had learned on reaching St. Petersburg was that Alexander had been astounded when he heard that Napoleon was heading towards the ancient and sacred Capital of Russia.

He had never imagined that the Emperor would actually attempt to march to Moscow and the thought of the inevitable carnage appalled him.

The one blessing from the Russian point of view, the Duke told himself, was the fact that the Czar was not himself leading the Russian Armies.

His record as a Military leader had been so disastrous that even now every setback was attributed to his influence.

Because his sister had been so desperate, she had written to him bluntly in a manner that no one else would have dared to do,

"For God's sake, do not decide to assume command yourself. There is no time to lose to give the Armies a Chief in whom the men will have confidence. As for you, you cannot inspire them with any."

Amazingly, Alexander had heeded her pleas and left the Army.

He had travelled back to Moscow, then to St. Petersburg. Everywhere he heard criticisms of the High Command and everywhere there was a cry for Kutuzov, whose name spelt magic for the people.

Alexander had no faith in General Kutuzov. He felt that he was a figure from another century, but he decided to bow to popular demand and told the Duke on his arrival,

"The public want him so I have appointed him. As for me I wash my hands of the whole affair!"

The Duke understood that he was feeling peeved at being more or less deposed in favour of a sixty-seven year old General who was lazy, licentious and knew nothing about modern warfare.

Other people in The Winter Palace, however, informed the Duke that Kutuzov, despite all his shortcomings, had the common sense born of long years of experience.

"He is slow but tenacious," an elderly statesman said, "lazy, but discerning, impassive but cunning."

All this information the Duke conveyed in code by special Courier to London.

He hoped with one of his more mocking smiles that the Prime Minister and the Foreign Minister would be able to make something out of it.

'The one thing about Russia,' he told himself, 'is that the unexpected always happens and at least there is nothing monotonous here in day to day life.'

He realised that he was enjoying himself in his own rather cynical fashion and with that thought in his mind he fell into a deep sleep.

*

At nine o'clock the Duke was admitted to the Czar's private apartments.

To get there he walked through what seemed to him to be miles of the most beautiful and finely decorated rooms that he had ever seen in his whole life.

He had been quite prepared for magnificence for the stories of St. Petersburg's treasures and the splendour of its buildings had been told and retold in London.

It had been the extravagant Empress Elizabeth who had pulled down the original wooden Winter Palace built by Peter the Great and her architect, Rastrelle, in eight years covered an area of two million square feet with over one thousand rooms and one hundred staircases.

The Empress Catherine, when she came to power, commissioned a Summer Palace that would outshine Versailles and in St. Petersburg she had added three buildings to the immense Winter Palace, which were known as 'The Hermitage'.

Between the two buildings there were courtyards heated in winter where rare birds flitted amongst the trees and shrubberies.

The Empress had instructed her Ambassadors in Paris, Rome and London to keep a sharp lookout for art bargains and they bought her plenty of fine pictures by great Masters such as Rembrandt, Tiepolo, Van Dyck and Poussin.

The Duke glanced only perfunctorily at these magnificent works of art for his mind was still concerned with Bonaparte's advance into Russia.

'It would be a tragedy,' he told himself, 'if treasures such as I see here should be lost to posterity.'

When he reached the Czar's apartments, he was saluted by the sentries of the Grenadiers of the Golden Guard.

Picked for their great height, out of all the Regiments who wore the Russian bearskins, they were the most gorgeous.

They wore white trousers and leggings, a black tunic with gold cuffs and collar and cutaway tails, gold-edged with red on which was fastened a cartridge case embossed with a double-headed eagle.

The Duke found the Czar waiting for him. Tall, fair-haired and externally handsome it was easy to understand that the Russian people had looked at Alexander on his accession like a Fairytale King come to save them from all their miseries.

Yet when, at twenty-four years of age, he had ridden to his Coronation in 1801, a wit in St. James's had remarked,

"He was preceded by men who had murdered his grandfather, escorted by men who had murdered his father and followed by men who would not think twice about murdering him!"

The Duke had heard from one of the Czar's closest friends that, when Alexander had learned of his father's cruel death, he had burst into tears.

"I have not the strength to reign," he had sobbed to his wife. "Let someone else take my place"

The Duke had begun to think that the vision of Paul's strangled battered body haunted the Czar.

He was perceptive enough to know that Russians could suffer in their souls in a way that perhaps men of other nations are unable to do.

He had known the Czar for some years personally and he was aware that he was often mentally convulsed with an inner agony that would, he thought, become worse rather than better as he grew older.

As he might have expected, the Czar was this morning looking worried and speaking in a manner that had a touch of hysteria about it.

"The news is bad – very bad!" he told the Duke after he had greeted him.

"What have you learned, Sire?" the Duke enquired.

"That Bonaparte is still marching towards Moscow!"

The Czar spoke as if he could hardly bear to say the words and then he sighed,

"God knows if it is the truth. To be honest no one seems to know what is happening."

The Duke was not astonished at this statement.

Methods of communication between the Army and the Czar were mostly haphazard and incompetent, as were a great many other things in Russia.

They sat down to breakfast at which, as was usual, there were three kinds of bread.

One was a roll of white bread called *kalatch*, as light as a feather and eaten hot, which was made from water brought especially from the River Moska.

This water was delivered to all the Palaces in St. Petersburg, a custom that dated from the previous century.

As they ate, the Czar, instead of talking about what was happening to the troops under Kutuzov's direction, did nothing but quote passages from the Bible.

When the Duke looked at him in surprise, he explained,

"Yesterday I was told that my lifelong friend, Prince Alexander Golitzen, is a traitor."

"That is impossible!" exclaimed the Duke, who knew the Prince quite well.

"I tried not to believe what I was told," the Czar said in a low voice, "but my informant said that he is constructing an impressive new Palace where he could entertain Napoleon."

"Surely you don't believe such a wild tale?" the Duke asked.

"I went at once to visit Golitzen and asked him point-blank why he had chosen to build in such troubled times."

"What was his reply?" the Duke asked.

"The Prince answered, 'Your Imperial Majesty need not fear an invasion if you trust in Divine Providence'."

The Duke raised his eyebrows, but made no comment and the Czar went on,

"Golitzen then reached up to a bookshelf to take down a heavy volume of the Bible. It slipped to the floor and fell open at the page on which is printed Psalm 41."

The Czar paused impressively and the Duke said,

"I am afraid, Sire, I have forgotten that particular Psalm."

"'*I will say of the Lord, He is my refuge and fortress, my God, in Him will I trust*'," the Czar quoted.

His voice had deepened and sounded impressive as he added,

"Golitzen convinced me that the opening of the Bible at this place was not a coincidence but a direct message from God."

"I hope the Prince was right," the Duke commented dryly.

"I am sure of it!" the Czar said. "All night I have been reading the Bible and meditating on God and our situation. I believe we will be saved."

The Duke found it difficult not to remark that the Russians would certainly need the help of the Almighty as they could not hope to rely entirely on their Army.

Before he left England, he had seen a report by Dr. Clarke, an Englishman who had paid a visit the Tula arms factory only two years earlier in 1810 and he had been appalled by the incompetence he found there.

His report said,

"The machinery is ill-constructed and worse preserved. Everything seemed out of order. Workmen with long beards stood staring at each other wondering what was to be done next, while their intendants or directors were either drunk or asleep. Notwithstanding all this, they pretended to issue thirteen hundred muskets a week from the manufactory!"

"What was the actual figure?" the Duke had asked.

"I have no idea," was the answer, "but we have learnt that the Russian muskets, besides being clumsy and heavy, misfire five times out of ten and are liable to burst when they are discharged."

The Duke had thought that French spies must have provided Napoleon Bonaparte with the same type of report as Dr. Clarke's.

On invading Russia he was doubtless anticipating that the resistance he would encounter would not be very effective against his forces, highly organised and armed as they were with the latest most up to date equipment.

It would, however, have been pointless and merely unkind to repeat any of this to the Czar. So the Duke did his best to talk of other things, knowing that there was nothing to be gained by having 'The Little Father' of such a great country in such depths of despair.

'Perhaps things will turn out better than I anticipate,' he told himself optimistically.

But he found, when he moved amongst the Royal Family and other people staying in the Winter Palace, that they were as apprehensive as he was.

He also found the whole atmosphere so depressing that he decided to call on Princess Ysevolsov whom he had known for many years.

He had found when he arrived at The Winter Palace, a letter written in her usual animated and flowery manner, begging him to take the first opportunity he could find of renewing their friendship.

"*My poor husband is, of course, away on the Battlefield,*" she wrote, *but I will receive you with open arms as one of my closest and dearest friends in England and I want too for you to meet my Little Tania. She was only ten or eleven when you last saw her. Now she is very beautiful and, when this tiresome War is over, I want to present her to our friends in London and have her make her curtsey to the Queen at Buckingham Palace.*"

The Duke had read the letter and found quite a lot of information written 'between the lines'. He knew that Prince Ysevolsov was one of the richest men in Russia. His family, like other members of the Nobility for some generation's past not only owned huge estates but a fantastic number of serfs.

Prince Ysevolsov, the Duke remembered, was supposed to own twenty-five thousand serfs in different Provinces of the country.

He not only used them as goldsmiths, carpenters and ebony carvers but for his private theatrical company and his *Corps de Ballet*.

He had his own theatre where he gave performances for his friends and his wife was as beautiful and valuable as his other possessions.

She had, however, both Austrian and English blood in her and she had often said to the Duke that she hoped that her children, when they grew up, would not marry Russians.

The Duke, with his retentive memory, had now a very good idea why she was pressing upon him the attractions of her daughter Tania.

It would, in fact, be a very suitable match for the daughter of one of the richest and most important Noblemen in Russia to marry one of the richest and most prestigious Noblemen of England.

But the Duke told himself that the Princess would be disappointed. He was now thirty-three and had so far evaded matrimony.

Although he had come perilously near to being swept up the aisle from time to time, he had always at the last moment extracted himself from a difficult position.

In the past few years he had ensured that the danger did not occur by having little or nothing to do with young girls.

His love affairs were always conducted with married women or widows and he made it clear from the beginning of his acquaintance with the widows that he preferred his bachelor freedom.

"You will have to marry one day to have a son."

It was a sentence that was repeated and re-repeated to him until he told himself that, as far as he was concerned, the Dukedom could go to his younger brother and his family without it causing him one qualm of regret.

The more he saw of the women who had made London under the Prince of Wales, now the Prince Regent, the gayest and one of the most promiscuous Cities in the world, the more he was determined that love affairs were one thing but marriage was most certainly another.

He had no intention of marrying a woman who would be unfaithful to him and disliked the idea of having to deceive his wife or to lie in an effort to protect himself.

He knew that he was too proud and had too much integrity to wish to debase himself in any way least of all by falsehood and deception.

"I shall never marry," the Duke had said not once but a thousand times.

He thought now that it would be a pity if he could no longer indulge in such delightful intrigues such as the one that had happened last night without experiencing a somewhat guilty conscience the following morning.

As it was, he imagined with amusement, that either the Czar or someone in the Foreign Ministry would undoubtedly be now asking Katharina what she had learned from him the night before.

And, although he was certain that with her agile mind, she would give them something to chew over and he had said nothing to her that could not have been published in every Russian newspaper that existed.

He had seen Katharina in the distance at luncheon looking alluringly attractive in a gown that was definitely Parisian and wearing fantastic jewels, which he was certain had not been given to her by her aged and fortunately absent husband.

Their eyes had met for just one moment across the Reception room into which they had moved when the meal was over.

She told the Duke without words that she wanted him and he had only to lift his finger for her to be at his side.

What she signalled, however, made the Duke decide that before he concerned himself once again with their fiery love-making, he should extend his knowledge of St. Petersburg and perhaps find out from outside The Winter Palace what other people were thinking.

Accordingly he walked down the magnificent marble stairway with its white and gold pillars to the front door.

Here he ordered one of the *drotskis* that were always at the disposal of the Czar's guests and, having given instructions to be taken to the Ysevolsov Palace, set off in the sunshine.

Even for August it was very hot and there was just a little breeze coming from the river although there was a touch of salt in the air.

The enormously wide roads laid out by Peter the Great had practically no traffic on them at this time of the day when most people preferred to remain at home, and anyway, owing to the ominous news, there was less entertaining than usual.

As he drove along, the Duke enjoyed looking at the magnificent Palaces and buildings so different in their brilliant colours to the grey Palladians of England.

The Roumainzov Palace was painted orange, the Ministry of Justice blue, the enormous Pavlovski Barracks designed for Czar Paul was yellow.

The Duke was most interested in the *Manège de la Garde à Cheval*. It was painted green and had a portico of eight Doric columns of white granite.

With his great knowledge of horseflesh, the Duke had already admired the black horses of the *Gardes à Cheval*, the chestnuts of the *Chevaliers Gardes* and the dapple greys of the Gatchina Hussars.

The *drotski* drawn by two excellent horses reached the Ysevolsov Palace within five minutes.

The Duke entered the hallway, which if not as magnificent as that in The Winter Palace, could certainly stand comparison with any house he had visited elsewhere in the world.

A footman took him up the grand marble staircase, which divided and rose to a landing ornamented with exquisite specimens of Chinese porcelain.

They passed through a huge Reception room so large that two hundred people or more could easily be entertained in it without crowding.

The Duke expected to be asked to wait, but the footman, speaking in hesitating French, explained,

"*Madame la Princesse* is in the theatre, *monsieur.*"

The Duke nodded his understanding and they then walked on again through a number of magnificently decorated rooms until, in the centre of one of them, they reached a staircase made of priceless malachite descending to the floor below.

The Duke had heard in England that Prince Ysevolsov's private theatre was exceptional, but he was not prepared for the utmost beauty of what he saw when the servant opened a gold-encrusted door and he was shown in to what was obviously a Royal Box.

Very small and holding fewer than a hundred people, it was like a child's doll's house in a Royal Mansion and yet it had all the charm and the beauty of an Imperial theatre.

In the stalls there were white and gold carved chairs. The circle was supplied with seats in crimson velvet, as was the box he had entered.

The footman had not announced him and he stood at the back noting that in front of him was the figure of the Princess, who had not heard his arrival as she was intent on watching what was taking place on the stage.

A girl was dancing to the music of a small orchestra seated in the pit below.

The Duke glanced at the performer perfunctorily. He then assumed with the Prince's obsession for the theatre that it would be either a member of his own special *Corps de Ballet* giving a performance or else, what was more likely, one of his family.

At the back of his mind he remembered the Princess or someone else telling him that the Prince himself enjoyed acting and expected his family to perform with him.

If there was one thing that the Duke really disliked, it was amateur theatricals and he hoped what was taking place would not continue for too long as he wanted to talk to the Princess.

Then the girl who was dancing made a deep curtsey.

'Thank goodness!' the Duke sighed to himself.

He was just about to move forward to make his presence known to his hostess, when the girl, and he could see that she was very pretty, ran from the stage and the music changed and another performer appeared.

She was moving on the tips of her toes and wearing the traditional ballet skirt worn by those who took part in *Les Sylphides*.

It reached to her ankles and there was a tight bodice, low-cut to display a long swan-like neck and her bare arms.

The Duke mused impatiently that the new ballet that he had seen performed the previous evening in Catherine the Great's theatre in The Winter Palace had rather bored him.

Then he realised that it was not the music of that ballet and he had not heard it before, also the movements of the dancer on stage were exceptionally graceful.

Despite his irritation he found himself watching the way she moved.

He had a feeling that the dance was not traditional or, if it was, he had never seen it before.

He knew too that the music, while strange, was particularly tuneful and had a melodious beauty about it that intrigued him.

The Duke, like the Prince Regent, was very fond of music. As in everything else that he was really interested in, he was a connoisseur and a very discriminating one.

Now he knew that he was listening to an exceptionally fine work that did not sound to him in the least Russian.

Then, as he watched the girl moving around the stage, dancing with a spontaneity and a kind of joy that he had never seen expressed before, he was sure, although he had no reason for it, that she too was unusual.

He could not explain why she seemed different, except that, as far as he was concerned, she was original both in her movements, in her grace and in her dance.

'Russia is full of surprises,' he told himself and found that the music of the dance evoked some response in him that he had not felt for a very long time.

Earlier, when he was young, he had been deeply moved not only by music but also by poetry until, like everything else in his life, it had grown far too familiar. He had found that, while he appreciated the subtleties of such things, they no longer aroused him as they had in his youth.

Now oddly and almost inexplicably he felt his mind, or was it something deeper, flying as if it had wings on the music as his eyes watched the grace and joy expressed by the dancer.

It seemed to him as if she moved amongst trees covered with blossom and the whole world was awakening with spring.

There was something young and creative about her and the Duke thought that he saw butterflies hovering around her and birds in the sky above.

It was almost with a sense of loss when he realised that the dance was over as the dancer swept to the ground in the traditional curtsey and the music came to an end.

Two red velvet curtains fell and then rose as the two girls came forward hand in hand to take a final bow.

There was only the Princess to clap her hands, but she did so with enthusiasm.

"Excellent," she called out. "Both of you were very good. Go and change and come to the White Salon."

The two girls then slipped away through the curtains and for the first time the Princess became aware that the Duke was standing behind her in the box.

She gave a little cry of delight and, rising, held out both her hands.

"Blake!" she cried. "You have come and I am so very pleased to see you."

"As I to see you, Sonya," the Duke answered. "Who were those entrancing creatures? They held me spellbound."

"The first was Tania, my little Tania, whom I so much want you to meet," the Princess replied. "You will see her in a few moments and I know that you will believe everything I have told you about her and so much more."

The Princess linked her arm through the Duke's as she spoke and led him through the door at the back of the box.

As they started to climb the malachite staircase, the Duke asked,

"And the other dancer?"

There was a quite perceptible pause before the Princess replied,

"Oh, that was Zoia!"

CHAPTER TWO

The Duke was about to ask Zoia's other name, but the Princess chattered on,

"You must find it terribly hot here as we all do. Of course ordinarily we are never in St. Petersburg at this time of the year but, as the Czar is at The Winter Palace, how can we go to the country and feel that we are deserting him?"

They moved through the beautiful apartments that the Duke had noted on his way to the theatre and footmen then opened the double doors of a huge Reception room, which the Duke realised was aptly named as it was all in white.

The carved stone mantelpiece was an artistic delight and the curtains under the exquisite gold pelmets were of heavy white Chinese silk.

There was a glittering silver teapot on a silver tray set on a low table by one of the sofas and the Princess laughed when she saw the Duke's expression.

"English tea at five o'clock," she said. "I became acclimatised to it in England and now a number of people in St. Petersburg have followed my example. I cannot offer you muffins, but I think you will find the little *blini* to your taste."

As these were, the Duke knew, small buckwheat pancakes that were filled with caviar and sour cream, he could reply quite truthfully that they were indeed very much to his taste.

He sat down in a comfortable chair and waited for the cup of tea that the Princess poured out in the same manner that his mother had dispensed tea in England.

"How long are you staying?" she asked, "or have you not yet made up your mind?"

"I rather feel that the news from the Front might decide that for me," the Duke replied.

The Princess shrugged her shoulders.

"Now we have Kutuzov everything will be all right and our Army will win!"

The Duke felt that she was being slightly over-optimistic, but at least it was a change from the despondency at The Winter Palace, so he merely answered,

"I hope you are right. You should come and talk to the Czar."

"It would do no good," the Princess replied. "You know as well as I do, Blake, that, if there is one thing that the Russians really enjoy, it is gloom and despondency whenever there is a crisis. My husband is the same, but with him I merely wait until the sun shines again."

The Duke laughed.

"An easy philosophy from a very lovely philosopher."

There was no doubt that he spoke the truth when he complimented the Princess.

She had been, when the Prince married her, the most outstanding beauty in the Court of Vienna and age had improved rather than detracted from her looks.

There was, however, a forcefulness about her that made the Duke suspect that she drove her husband and, in a very un-Russian manner, ruled the household.

Russians, for the most part, liked their women to be soft, feminine and unobtrusive, but the two famous Empresses, Elizabeth and Catherine the Great, had set a standard which many Russian wives followed by being irritatingly dictatorial.

The Princess, however, was not Russian and the Duke knew it amused her to decry the nation that she had married into very simply because she wished, as it were, to challenge her husband's importance.

The Prince was a good-natured easy-going man. He liked peace in his home and peace for his country and the Duke was sure that if he was now playing the part of a soldier at the moment it was reluctantly and only from a sense of patriotism.

The Princess was talking about London and asking questions about her friends when the door opened and the two girls, whom the Duke had seen dancing, came into the room.

There was little doubt that Tania, who led the way, was just as pretty as her mother's description of her.

She had dark hair and a white skin, large eyes set well apart and a full smiling mouth.

As she curtseyed to the Duke, he was sure that, when she came to London, she would be a social success.

Then he heard the Princess saying,

"And this is Zoia. She came with us here from Moscow so that Tania could improve her French."

For the first time since she had entered the room the Duke looked at the girl he had seen dancing on the stage and who had mysteriously affected him in a manner that he did not wish to remember.

He was sure that it had been just an illusion engendered by the heat of the day or perhaps a delayed reaction from the wine he had drunk at luncheon.

Whatever the cause, he did not wish to recall it and he had been quite certain that, when he met Zoia face to face, he would realise that it was just a fantasy of his mind and had, in fact, little to do with the performance.

A slight figure curtseyed gracefully in front of him.

Then, as she rose, she lifted her face to his and he found himself looking into eyes that seemed in some extraordinary way to have purple depths in them.

As he looked into Zoia's face, the Duke realised that she was different from any other woman he had ever met.

It was not that she was beautiful, a great many women were that. It was not that she was particularly striking and her loveliness was not as obvious as that of Tania.

But there was indeed something in the almost classical features, the little straight nose, the perfect curve of the lips and the oval of the face, which reminded the Duke of the statuary he had seen in Greece and some of the very fine examples that he owned himself amongst his other treasures.

He thought too as he looked at her that, while she was flesh and blood, she had the purity and the exclusiveness of the statues that had once been worshipped by those who appreciated their sanctity.

That, he told himself in an almost startled manner, was the right word to describe Zoia.

There was something sacred about her and he thought for one moment that there was a light behind her or that it came from within her as she stood facing him.

He realised that they were looking at each other, that Zoia's eyes were held by his and that both of them were very still.

The Princess's voice suddenly seemed to come from a long way away.

"Sit down, children," she urged, "and hurry with your tea. I want to talk to His Grace, who is a very old friend, and we prefer to be alone."

She was pouring tea into a cup as she spoke and now she looked up and was aware that the Duke and Zoia had not moved.

In a voice that had a sharp edge to it, she added,

"I am sure, Zoia, it is time for you to practise your music. Go to the Music Room and tell the servants to bring your tea there. It will save time."

As the Princess spoke, Zoia gave a start as if she had been recalled from some distant place.

She gave the Princess and the Duke a little curtsey and then without speaking she left the room.

As the door closed behind her, the Duke had a sudden desire to call out to her to stay, and, when she was gone, he had an unaccountable feeling of loss because she was no longer there.

"Do come and sit down, Blake," the Princess suggested, "and tell my little Tania about London. She has not been there since she was ten, but she has the happiest memories of your Parks and the funny narrow little streets."

The Duke realised that the Princess's description of London was due to the fact that the streets of St. Petersburg were so wide and so sparsely inhabited.

Because Tania was looking at him in an expectant manner, he asked genially,

"Are you really looking forward to visiting London? I can assure you it is not half so grand or as impressive as St. Petersburg."

"Mama tells me that I shall attend balls in London that are more amusing than those that take place here."

"That I find difficult to believe," the Duke replied, "with so many handsome and dashing young Officers to partner you."

"Not at the moment," Tania answered. "They are all away fighting the French and there are far too many women at every party."

She pouted as she spoke and the Duke laughed.

"Let's hope for your sake, if for nobody else's, that the War will be over soon."

"War! War! War!" the Princess groaned. "Do we ever hear about anything else? I had planned such delightful parties for Tania at The Summer Palace and now all we can do is to stay here in this heat."

"I can only say how sorry I am for you," the Duke said with a slightly cynical note in his voice.

He thought that it was typical of the Princess to ignore the huge casualties that there had been at the Battle of Smolensk.

"Let's talk of something more interesting," the Princess said with a swift change of mood before he could speak. "Now that you are here, I must give a party for you, a dinner party, and we will dance later to a new gypsy band I have discovered which is quite fantastic."

She smiled before she went on,

"I am keeping them secret in case they should appear at any party before mine, but you shall be my excuse to present them to an astonished St. Petersburg."

'Will the Czar approve?" the Duke asked. "After all he is very depressed and worried about the War."

"We will not invite him," the Princess said. 'We will tell everyone that it is just a quiet little dinner party for you, but all my special friends shall come and Tania and I will entertain you, will we not, dearest?"

She spoke to Tania whose eyes were alight with excitement.

"A party with dancing afterwards, Mama! It will be so thrilling. I was saying to Zoia only today how dull it is with nothing to look forward to."

"You have your ballet dancing," the Duke reminded her.

Tania shrugged her shoulders.

"I have had lessons for years to please Papa, but Zoia dances so much better than I do."

"Zoia comes into another category altogether," the Princess said coldly. "Now run along, darling, and I will let you come back and say 'goodbye' to the Duke before he leaves."

"I should like that," Tania said with what was almost a coquettish glance at the Duke.

She curtseyed and ran from the room and the Princess watched her go.

Then she turned and asked,

"What do you think of her, Blake?"

"I think she is extremely pretty just like her mother," the Duke replied, "and she will be a triumphant success amongst the beaux of St James's."

"I would like her to be a success with you," the Princess said softly.

"Me?" the Duke enquired in a voice which proclaimed that he had never thought of such an idea. "You know that I am a confirmed bachelor. Besides I am much too old for anything so young and lovely."

"I think Tania would be happier with an older man," the Princess parried seriously. "She needs guidance. She also at times needs a firm hand."

"Have you ever wondered what I should have in common with a child who has only just left the schoolroom?" the Duke asked. "No, my dear Sonya, my interests are very much more sophisticated."

He spoke deliberately in a way that made it seem a compliment and there was, as he had intended, a sudden alertness in the Princess's eyes as she put out one of her heavily ringed hands towards him.

"You know as well as I do, Blake, that you typify everything that is handsome, gallant and attractive in an Englishman."

The Duke kissed her fingers as was expected.

Then he said,

"I promise you that all the most eligible bachelors shall be paraded before Tania when you bring her to London. In fact I think one of my younger brothers might suit her very well."

As he spoke, he saw that the Princess was calculating that, if he never married, as he said he had no intention of doing, then his brother would in the course of time become the Duke of Welminster and Tania would achieve the position that she wished for her.

Aloud she merely smiled,

"I knew I could rely on your kindness."

"Tell me about Tania's friend," the Duke asked. "She also seems to be quite a pretty girl. Will you be bringing her to London too?"

He deliberately made his voice sound uninterested and the Princess responded,

"Poor Zoia, I am so sorry for her. It is not her fault that things are as they are."

"What do you mean?" the Duke asked again in what he hoped was an uninterested voice.

"I forgot," the Princess said, "that I did not tell you who she was."

"And who is she?"

"She is Pierre Vallon's daughter."

For a moment the Duke could not think how he had heard the name.

Then he exclaimed,

"Do you mean the Conductor?"

"Of course," the Princess replied. "There is only one Vallon in the musical world and he now has a unique position."

"I heard him conducting in London last year," the Duke said, "and long ago when I was a boy in Paris. I suppose he is without exception one of the greatest Conductors in the world today and I have always thought that the music he composes is superlative."

As he spoke, he knew now why he had been so drawn to the music that Zoia had danced to and which had aroused such strange feelings within him.

"I had no idea that Vallon had a family," he added.

"You know his story, of course."

"As a matter of fact, I do not," the Duke replied. "I have admired and acclaimed him for his art and I suppose I never thought of him as a man."

"Then I will tell you," the Princess said.

The Duke knew, because she was an insatiable gossip that it pleased her to be able to impart to him something that he did not know already.

"Pierre Vallon's wife," she said, "was Natasha Strovolsky."

The Duke was startled as she had meant him to be.

"Strovolsky!" he exclaimed.

He was well aware that the Strovolsky family, one of the most important in Russia, were extremely proud of their Royal connections.

Wherever the Czar went, there was always one member of the family in attendance upon him by right not only as a Courtier but by birth because the same blood flowed in their veins.

The Strovolskys were so proud and so Imperial in their behaviour, that it was laughingly said that the Czar would wake up one morning to find a Strovolsky sitting on the Throne!

Without the Princess saying anything more the Duke knew that the idea of a member of the Strovolsky family marrying a French Conductor, however famous, was unthinkable.

"How can it be possible?" he asked.

But he knew that the Princess was only waiting for the question to begin her story.

"You will remember," she began, "that it was Gregory Orlov himself who put Catherine the Great on the Throne of Russia."

"Yes, of course," the Duke murmured.

Count Orlov, as he became, was part of Russian history.

He was extremely handsome, insatiably ambitious and Europe had in 1762 learnt with astonishment that due to his machinations a German Princess of petty origin had snatched the Crown of Russia first from Czar Peter III and then from Peter's son, Paul.

The Duke had heard her described as 'not only a murderess but a usurper, not only a usurper but a whore'.

The Duke's father, who had visited Russia at that time, had often told him how obsessed the Empress, an autocrat with everyone else, had been with her lover, Orlov.

"I believe the fellow beats her in private," the old Duke had said, "but she is passionately in love with him and I have never seen anything like the presents that have been heaped upon him."

The Duke remembered now that his father had described a suit that the Count had worn on which was sewn a million pounds worth of diamonds and told him of a fête at which the dessert at supper was set out with jewels to the value of over two million pounds sterling.

"Ten years after her Coronation," the Princess was continuing, "the Empress Catherine decided to replace Gregory Orlov as her lover."

The Duke smiled.

"Because he was having an affair with Princess Golitzena."

"Exactly," the Princess agreed. "But what the Empress did not know, nor at the time did anyone else, was that he had been briefly but passionately in love with the young Princess Petya Strovolsky."

"It seems incredible!" the Duke exclaimed.

"Incredible or not, you can imagine the horror when they discovered that their prettiest and most adored daughter was having a child."

The Princess made a gesture with her hands that was very eloquent before she continued,

"The Prince was an astute and, of course, all-powerful man. Very few people and only those closest to the family were aware of this lamentable and, indeed from their point of view, horrifying situation. They were not only humiliated by the position but terrified, as you can imagine, that the Empress would learn of it."

"What did they do?" the Duke asked.

"Petya was sent to stay with some friends in Austria, which was how I came to learn the sad story. Her child was born there and it was a daughter, who was christened Natasha."

The Duke was listening intently as the Princess carried on,

"A year later Petya and the baby returned to Russia and the Strovolskys accepted the baby, announcing that Petya had married a distant cousin who had died in Vienna."

"And they were believed?" the Duke enquired.

"But of course!" the Princess answered. "No one would dare to contradict any statement made by Prince Strovolsky."

"Then what happened?"

"Natasha was brought up with the family and then Petya married one of my husband's cousins and died in childbirth. Count Orlov was the love of her life and she never really cared for anybody else."

"I believe the Empress reinstated him, did she not?" the Duke asked.

"She would always say, 'I cannot be a day without love', for as a lover she missed him desperately. On his return she loaded him up with gifts, six thousand serfs, a salary of one hundred thousand roubles and Heaven knows what else."

"Am I mistaken in thinking that he gave her a gift of great importance?" the Duke asked.

"A superb solitaire diamond," the Princess replied. "It cost him four hundred thousand roubles and it is the most beautiful single gem in the world!"

The Duke registered in his mind that in the Empress Catherine's reign it was five roubles to the pound and that Orlov's gift was certainly an expressive apology.

"Go on with your story," he urged.

"You can imagine the consternation in the Strovolsky household after they had done everything they could to try to forget the anxiety and risk of humiliation and shame that Petya had brought on them, to discover then that her daughter, Natasha, had run away with their children's Tutor."

"So that was what Pierre Vallon was."

"He came to Russia like so many other Frenchmen to teach the children of the noble families to speak, to dance and to make music. You have seen him and so will understand that anyone who employed such a handsome man in a household full of young girls was asking for trouble."

The Duke agreed.

He had thought that Pierre Vallon, when he had seen him conducting at a huge party given by the Prince Regent at Carlton House, was not only outstandingly good-looking but had an inescapable charm that had made the ladies present fawn on him in a manner that had made their host quite jealous.

"What did Princess Natasha look like?" the Duke wanted to know.

"She was absolutely lovely," the Princess replied.

"Was?" the Duke questioned.

"She died a year ago and that is why I was so sorry for Zoia and brought her here from Moscow, while her father is conducting at the *Grand Theatre*, to give her a chance to forget what is inevitably a worse tragedy than for any other girl in similar circumstances."

"Why do you say that?" the Duke asked.

The Princess looked at him pityingly as if he was being rather stupid.

"While the Princess was alive, the child had some chance of meeting decent men, one of whom might have been inclined to ignore the consequences of marrying her, but now – "

The Princess's hands went out expressively.

" – now Zoia is just the daughter of a French Conductor."

"But a very famous one," the Duke pointed out, "and a composer whose work rates with that of the greatest Masters of music."

"However talented he may be," the Princess said coldly, "however delightful to meet, you know as well as I do, my dear Blake, that socially he is just a French Tutor who has achieved success in his own particular profession or trade."

She sighed.

"I am very sorry for Zoia and I am certain that now Natasha is dead the Strovolskys will no longer wish to know her, in fact they have already told me so. I cannot believe that she will find Paris very amusing at this moment with Bonaparte conscripting every eligible man over the age of fifteen into his infamous Army."

"I can see the position very clearly," the Duke remarked,

"I have made you understand how charitable I have been in having her here at all," the Princess said, "Tania is fond of her and at least the two girls amuse one another when there is so little entertainment taking place at the moment."

As if she was bored with the subject of Zoia, the Princess went on,

"Now let us make plans, Blake. Which evening can you escape from The Winter Palace? But give me a little time to make it a really festive occasion."

"I have a feeling we will be in the Czar's black book."

"Then tell someone to give him another Bible to read," the Princess retorted. "It is all over St. Petersburg that

Prince Golitzen has him immersed in the Holy Scriptures. Personally I am waiting until I am ready for the grave before I become really religious."

Before the Duke could reply a servant came into the room and said something in a low voice to the Princess.

"Oh, what a nuisance!" she exclaimed. "There is a Courier here from my husband not only bringing me news from the Front but requiring a number of papers that only I can find."

The Duke rose to his feet.

"Then I must leave. If you are writing to the Prince, please tell him how disappointed I am that we cannot meet."

"He will be disappointed too," the Princess replied. "He has always been fond of you, as you are well aware."

She waved the servant away and said to the Duke in a low voice,

"Come and see me tomorrow, Blake, and we will make plans. Also I have so much to tell you, but now there is no time,"

She spoke in a way that made the Duke look at her enquiringly.

Then, having glanced over her shoulder to make sure that the servant had left the room, she said in a low voice,

"Be careful of Katharina Bagration."

"Careful?" the Duke asked.

"She is very close to the Czar and it is well known that she helps the Foreign Ministry with their investigations."

The Duke was too polite to say that he knew this already.

"Thank you, dear Sonya," he said. "You have always been a kind and generous friend and I assure you I am very grateful."

He raised her hand to his lips and kissed it.

The Duke walked from the room to see waiting outside the door the Courier who had come from the Prince wearing a stained and dusty uniform and looking as if he had ridden a long distance without sleep.

As the servant showed the Courier into the White Salon, the Duke walked along the corridor in the direction of the staircase.

He had reached it and was just about to descend the stairs when he heard the sound of music coming from a room on the other side of the landing,

He hesitated for a moment and then, walking to the door, opened it.

The room was as magnificent as the others in the house.

There were huge pillars of a very rare marble, which supported an exquisitely painted oval ceiling and the walls were decorated with murals of Goddesses and cupids.

On a small platform there was a pianoforte and seated at it was Zoia playing a melody that the Duke seemed to recognise.

He entered the room, closing the door behind him, and walked slowly towards her and it seemed to him once again that she was enveloped with light.

She was so intent on what she was playing that only when he drew nearer did she glance up and see him.

She stopped playing, but she did not rise and once again their eyes met and it seemed as if neither of them could move.

At last, after what appeared to be a very long time, the Duke found his voice.

"Is that one of your father's compositions?"

"Yes."

Her voice was low and it had exactly the tone, he thought, that he might have expected of her.

"I have met your father."

There was a sudden brightness in her eyes almost as if they held the sunshine.

It was strange, the Duke thought, that her hair should be fair.

Then he recalled that Pierre Vallon was not dark like most Frenchmen and he imagined, although he was not sure, that he came from Normandy, where fair hair and blue eyes were as common as in England.

There was no doubt that Zoia must have her mother's eyes and yet they held none of the mystery that the Duke had always associated with Russian women.

Instead there was something that, just like her face, had a spiritual quality about it which was inescapable.

He walked forward to step onto the small dais and leant against the piano.

"Tell me about yourself," he asked.

She smiled.

"What do you wish to know?"

"How have you learnt to dance as I saw you dancing just now on the stage?"

She did not appear surprised and he thought that she must have seen him in the box when she and Tania took their bows in front of the curtain.

"When I was small," Zoia told him, "Mama and I used to watch Papa play for the *Corps de Ballet*."

"You went to the theatre?"

"Yes – in Paris or anywhere else where he was playing," she replied. "Mama always wanted to be with him and he liked her to be there."

Without her having to say anything more, the Duke knew that there had been a deep love between her father and mother.

He could understand that, because the Princess had given up so much for her love, she wanted always to be with the man who mattered to her so much more than all the pomp and circumstance that she had enjoyed in Russia.

"Because I wanted to dance just like the ladies in the ballet," Zoia was saying, "Mama arranged for me to have lessons from a famous ballerina who had retired."

"You dance very beautifully."

"I would like to believe that is true," Zoia replied, "but Papa's music, which he wrote for me, is so inspiring that, when I hear it played, I feel as if I am swept away into another world where there is only music and sunshine."

That is exactly what she had portrayed in her dancing, he mused and remembered how he had thought that he saw butterflies and birds fluttering around her and felt that she danced under the blossom of flowering trees.

Even as he considered it, he was startled to realise that what he must have been seeing was what was in Zoia's thoughts.

Almost as if he would confirm or refute the idea out of hand, he asked her,

"Tell me, do tell me exactly what you were thinking when just now, I was watching you dancing."

She did not seem at all surprised at his question. She merely looked away from him and he thought that she was not only racking her memory to recall what had happened but staring deep into her heart.

"That particular music of Papa's, which is part of a concerto," she said, "makes me think of – spring – the blossom on the trees, the birds nesting, the flowers – and the butterflies hovering over them."

The Duke was silent from sheer astonishment.

Then he said,

"I understand your mother is dead. What will you do with yourself when you leave St. Petersburg?"

"I have come only for a short visit," Zoia answered, "because Papa asked me to do so, but today I heard for the first time that the French Army may be marching towards Moscow."

"It is a possibility."

"Then I must be with Papa."

"Your father will be safe whoever is in Moscow," the Duke said soothingly. "Pierre Vallon is an international figure and music, as you know, has no nationality but is universal."

"That is true," Zoia smiled. "At the same time guns do not always hit the target that they are aimed at and, if there was fighting in Moscow, I would be very frightened that Papa might be injured."

"Do you think if you are with him you will be able to prevent it?" the Duke enquired.

"I shall pray that he will be safe," Zoia replied. "But I would wish to be at his side."

"I think it would be far better if your father came to St. Petersburg," the Duke suggested. "But I will find out exactly what the situation is when I return to The Winter Palace and I will let your hostess know."

"That is very kind of you."

She gave a little sigh.

"Perhaps I was wrong to come away and leave Papa alone, but he was so insistent that I should accept the Princess's kind invitation."

"You are happy here?"

The Duke did not miss the perceptible little pause before Zoia volunteered,

"I like being with Tania – she is a very sweet person."

Although her voice was warm she spoke almost as if Tania was a small child and she was looking after her.

"How old are you?" the Duke asked.

"I am nearly twenty."

It struck the Duke that in twenty years she must have seen in her travels with her father and mother a great deal of the world and would therefore be very much older in mind and in knowledge than her contemporaries.

"Play to me?" he then proposed.

"What would you like to hear?"

"Something your father has written," he replied, "and something that is your favourite too."

Zoia ran her fingers over the keys.

Her hands were small and perfectly proportioned and, as she looked down, her eyelashes were dark against her cheeks.

The Duke thought she resembled even more than she had done before the statues that had always aroused a more intimate response in him than pictures. He had in his possession some of the finest pictures in England painted by great artists from every country in Europe, but whenever he returned to one of his houses it was his statuary that delighted him most.

Now he thought that the Aphrodite that stood in his house in Hampshire and, which had been brought back centuries ago from Greece by one of his ancestors, was more like Zoia than any of the canvases of the Madonnas, the Venuses or the angels hanging on the walls.

As she began to play, the Duke knew that, incredibly in a manner that he could not begin to understand, he was reading her thoughts and feeling within himself her response to the music.

It was winter and the Duke could see the snow on the ground, the trees white with frost and a stretch of frozen water.

It was beautiful, but cold and impersonal and apart from human needs.

Then imperceptibly, so for a moment he sensed rather than saw it, the sky brightened.

There was light, then the first glimmer of the sun and slowly the snow melted, the blue stillness of the ice broke and became a moving stream, the frost fell from the trees and the branches came to life.

There were the green buds of spring and the first white snowdrops and crocuses in the grass beneath them.

It was all in the rhythm, the smooth melody of the music and yet to the Duke it was as vivid as if he saw it happening in front of him. He could almost feel the warmth of the sunshine, smell the scent of the flowers as they bloomed one after another and then see the blossom fashion itself in the trees.

Next there was not only nature in what he saw, but someone human coming through the trees and moving towards him and he knew that she sought him as he waited for her.

She came nearer and nearer and he felt, as she did so, that his whole being went out towards her.

As he reached out, not only with his arms, but with his very soul, everything vanished.

There was silence and with a start that seemed to shake his whole body, he realised that Zoia was sitting at the piano, looking at him, her hands in her lap.

"Did you – like it – Your Grace?"

There was just a touch of anxiety in her soft voice as if she found it hard to understand why he had not spoken and why he was looking at her so strangely.

"Very much!"

The Duke heard his voice coming as if from a long distance away.

"I am glad – but I don't play as well as – Papa does."

"What does your father – call it?"

It was still very difficult for the Duke to speak. He felt as if his voice was constrained and was no longer his own.

"Papa called it *The Melting of the Ice*," Zoia answered. "There is a great deal more of the composition – but I thought perhaps you might be – bored."

The Duke wanted to say that she had no right to stop when she had. He had wanted her to go on. He had wanted to know what would happen when she touched the person for whom she had been waiting.

Then he told himself that, if he said such a thing, she would think he was mad. And yet he was not sure, she might understand.

He realised that she was waiting for him to say something, but before he could speak, she said,

"I think you – understood what Papa was – trying to say."

"Why should you think that?" he enquired.

"I don't know exactly," she replied simply. "But I felt while I was playing that it was not – just the music you heard – but something else."

Quite suddenly the Duke felt that he was bewitched and he was not sure that he liked it.

"I must go now," he said sharply. "Thank you, Miss Vallon, for playing for me. I am sure your father must be very proud of you."

Even as he spoke, he knew that he had disappointed her, but she politely rose to her feet and curtseyed.

"Goodbye."

He wanted to go and yet he wanted to stay. He did not understand himself.

"Goodbye – Your Grace."

The words were very low, but she did not look at him.

There was so much he wanted to ask and yet he did not want to hear the answers.

Abruptly, because he was disturbed out of his usual calm blasé attitude, he walked across the room towards the door.

Only as he reached it did he look back to see that Zoia was still standing at the piano.

She was not looking after him as any other woman would have done. Instead she was staring down at the keyboard and once again he had the feeling that he had disappointed her.

He went from the room closing the door gently behind him.

As he walked down the stairs, he told himself again that everything he had felt was an illusion and something to do with the heat.

His *drotski* was waiting and, as he drove back towards The Winter Palace, he thought that in some weird manner he had become immersed in the emotional dramatics of Russians who veered from elation to depression like a seesaw.

Yet that explanation did not hold good, because he was neither depressed nor elated.

Instead he had only felt something so strange that he could not explain it even to himself.

It had startled him out of a complacency in which he had believed for some years now that there was nothing new under the sun and very certainly nothing emotional that he had not tried in one way or another.

'I can hardly be becoming psychic in my old age!' the Duke thought to himself almost savagely.

It was fashionable in London to consult fortune-tellers and mediums and the Duke had heard that both Napoleon and his wife Josephine were fanatically superstitious.

It was well known that the Empress had been told when she was a girl in Martinique that she would occupy the highest position in France.

English Generals would relate scornfully that Napoleon consulted soothsayers before he embarked on a battle and was not above taking his revenge out on anyone who predicted bad luck.

The Duke had always thought that all such omens were a lot of nonsense practised only by charlatans who wished to obtain money in a fraudulent manner.

He had stayed at various houses over the years that were reputed to be haunted by ghosts and on more than one occasion had occupied what was known as 'the ghost room'.

"How did you sleep last night?" his host would ask breathlessly when he appeared at breakfast time.

"Absolutely peacefully," the Duke would reply with some relish. "I was not disturbed the whole night. In fact your ghost took not the slightest interest in me!"

His attitude was always deflating and he was equally contemptuous of those who carried a talisman at a Race Meeting or those of the theatrical profession who insisted on having a hare's foot in their dressing rooms.

'Good or bad luck is all in the mind,' he had said often enough. 'We make our Fate and our destiny is in our own hands.'

Now he asked himself how it was possible that he, of all people, could be beguiled not once but twice into not exactly seeing a vision but of feeling someone else's thoughts.

Being aware of them to the point where they were just as real as the setting sun gleaming iridescent on the waters of the River Neva and the statues on the roof of The Winter Palace silhouetted against the evening sky.

'I am either drunk or going mad' the Duke told himself irritably.

But he knew that it was neither of these.

'The sooner I forget such nonsense and get down to work the better,' he thought as he stepped out of the *drotski* and went up the steps into The Winter Palace.

He decided that he would find out what was the latest news from the Front and spend at least an hour coding a long communiqué to Lord Castlereagh in London.

A Courier could take it from him first thing in the morning and at least he would justify his stay in St. Petersburg.

He walked into the hall and handed his hat to an attendant footman. Then an Officer of the Grenadiers of the Golden Guard, who were on duty in the hall and along the corridors, came towards him.

"Good evening, Your Grace," he began in French. "The Princess Katharina Bagration would be grateful if you could visit her before you retire to your rooms."

"Of course," the Duke replied. "I shall be delighted to see Her Highness."

The Officer instructed a servant to escort him to the Princess's apartments.

As he followed the man, the Duke thought that Katharina would bring him down to earth and disperse all his ridiculous fantasies.

The one thing about Katharina was that she was extremely human, passionate, fiery and demanding, which were all emotions that the Duke could understand and feelings that he was thoroughly cognisant of.

'That is what I want,' he told himself, 'and nothing, *no nothing else*!'

CHAPTER THREE

The Duke half-expected to find Katharina alone, but when the footman showed him into a large formal Reception room redolent with flowers, he found that there were a number of other people present.

Katharina, looking extremely beautiful in a gown of blue gauze, moved towards him and he knew by the expression in her eyes how pleased she was to see him.

He kissed her hand and then he went immediately to greet the Czarina, who was standing next to the Czar.

Elizabeth Feodorovna would have been extremely attractive and a fitting mate for the handsome Alexander, only unfortunately she had a most unbecoming scurvy on her face.

The Duke, however, had always found her charming and far more emotionally stable than her husband.

He had only spoken to her for a few minutes when the Czar interrupted them.

"I have something to tell you, Welminster," he said, leading the Duke a little aside from the other people in the room.

The Duke looked at him apprehensively, but thought he seemed in a far better mood than he had been yesterday.

The despondency that made him seem to shrink into himself and become less imposing had gone and instead he was the commanding figure that he appeared to the Russians when he was on Parade.

"What is it, Sire?" the Duke asked.

"I know that all will be well," the Czar replied to him impressively. "Russia will conquer Napoleon and there is no longer any need for alarm."

The Duke looked at him incredulously and the Czar went on,

"This morning I had a direct message, which told me that my fears and my anxiety had been quite groundless."

"A message from the Front, Sire?"

"No, from God Himself," the Czar replied.

The Duke waited, wondering if anyone in England would believe this conversation if he recounted it in a despatch.

"I passed a night of terrible apprehension," the Czar began, "until at dawn I went to the window to look out and a voice told me to search in my Bible for inspiration."

He took a deep breath as if he was remembering every detail of what had happened to him.

"I put my finger into the Holy Book," he continued, "and it then pointed to a phrase that answered all my problems in just a few words."

'What did it say, Sire?" the Duke asked, knowing that this question was expected of him.

"*Arise and shine for thy light is come and the glory of the Lord is risen upon thee*," the Czar quoted.

There was an exaltation in his voice that was unmistakable and the Duke thought that here was another example of Russian mysticism and, as far as he was concerned, he had had enough of them.

"I am glad, Sire, that it brought you so much comfort," he said and found it difficult to prevent the cynicism sounding in his voice.

As if she sensed that the Duke was walking on dangerous ground, Katharina joined them.

"You are not allowed to talk secrets at my party, Sire," she said gaily to the Czar, "and I am longing to hear what happened when our English friend called on Princess Ysevolsov."

The Duke looked amused.

He knew that this was Katharina's way of informing him that she was well aware of where he had been and, if he thought that he could sneak out of The Winter Palace and no one know it, he was much mistaken!

"What did you expect to happen?" he asked.

Katharina looked at him from under her long eyelashes.

"I wondered for one thing whether you met the *Ice Maiden* and what you thought of her."

"The *Ice Maiden*?" the Duke questioned.

"Are you referring to Vallon's daughter?" the Czar enquired. "I was told that she had arrived in St. Petersburg."

"She is staying with Princess Ysevolsov, Sire," Katharina answered, "and I am sure that she has left many aching hearts behind in Moscow."

"Why is the lady in question called the *Ice Maiden*?" the Duke asked.

Katharina laughed.

"The Grand Duke Boris can give you a very plausible explanation for that," she replied.

"That is true," the Czar agreed. "I hear that the pavement outside the Vallon house in Moscow is worn thin with his constant pacing up and down."

"But the door is always barred to him," Katharina explained with a shriek of laughter, "and now the bird has flown, I am certain that the Grand Duke is, at this moment in time, in the depths of despair."

"I find it difficult to follow what you are saying," the Duke remarked in a disagreeable voice.

"It is not really very difficult," Katharina replied. "The Grand Duke is obsessed by Zoia Vallon and has been from the first moment he saw her. But knowing his reputation, first her mother and then her father barred him from the house and Boris is not used to being outside in the cold."

"It will do him good!" the Czar observed and moved away to speak to someone else.

The Duke thought the same thing. Equally he felt unexpectedly angry at the thought of the Grand Duke besmirching anyone so pure as Zoia.

For some reason that he could not account for, it had not occurred to him that her beauty would attract men, especially men like the Grand Duke.

She had seemed a creature apart from all the intrigues and machinations of the Social world, which were always the same in whatever country he found himself.

But now he began to understand why Pierre Vallon had insisted on his daughter leaving Moscow and coming to St. Petersburg under the chaperonage of Princess Ysevolsov.

She would be well aware, as the Duke was, what kind of person the Grand Duke was. A playboy, promiscuous and always in aggressive pursuit of some woman.

He was a byword wherever he went for his notorious love affairs and his extravagant behaviour.

When he was young, he had married a dull and unattractive German Princess whom he left with their children on his country estate and made sure that she seldom appeared either in St. Petersburg or Moscow.

That left him free to stalk like a hungry wolf amongst the lovely women who surrounded the Czar and who had made the Russian Court one of the most attractive that the Duke had ever visited.

It was ridiculous for him, he told himself harshly, to criticise the Grand Duke when his own reputation left much to be desired and his love affairs were gossiped about in England and had doubtless lost nothing in the telling in St. Petersburg.

Equally he could easily understand Vallon's alarm at the Grand Duke approaching his daughter.

He was quite certain that Princess Natasha, before she died, had been especially afraid of the consequences of a man with his reputation showing a partiality for a very young girl.

As if she knew where his thoughts were leading him, Katharina said to the Duke,

"Boris is Boris and we all know exactly what he is like. And after all the *Ice Maiden* might do worse for herself."

"Are you now suggesting that a girl as young as she is should accept the protection of the Grand Duke when his reputation stinks to high Heaven?"

The Duke spoke so violently that Katharina looked at him in surprise.

"I had no idea that you had such an animosity against Boris," she said. "Personally his *affaires de coeur* don't worry me. And for the sake of argument what alternative is there for the daughter of a French musician?"

"Good Heavens!" the Duke exclaimed. "Both you and Sonya Ysevolsov speak as if he was the trombone player in some sleazy orchestra! The man is a genius. I have never seen the Prince Regent so moved or so enthusiastic as when he played at Carlton House."

Katharina shrugged her shoulders.

"I grant you that his music is good and he has had a great success in the music world, but we are talking about his daughter, the *Ice Maiden*."

"That is what I hope she is where the Grand Duke is concerned!"

"From all I have heard she indeed offers him no encouragement," Katharina replied, "but perhaps she is secretly in love with some unimportant suitor her father has no knowledge of."

The Duke was about to reply that he was quite certain that Zoia would deceive no one, least of all her father, because it was not in her nature.

Then he thought that by saying so, he would be making a fool of himself over a girl whom he had seen once and who he knew nothing about.

What did it matter to him who pursued her, wooed her or offered her protection?

Even as he argued with himself, he realised that everything in him that was decent and every remnant of his reverence for women, revolted at the thought of anything so spiritual and exquisite being pressured, because there was no alternative, into an immoral association.

He had an impulse to see Vallon and discuss the problem of his daughter's future with him and to advise him for instance to take her to England where she would doubtless be more readily accepted than in caste-ridden Russia.

There was no snobbery in the world, the Duke thought, greater than in the Society that centred around the Czar.

He knew that both Sonya Ysevolsov and Katharina Bagration were right when they said that there was no possible chance of anyone of her mother's breeding offering Zoia marriage.

Yet the Duke found it impossible to think of her stepping down from the pedestal on which he had placed her to become soiled and besmirched by the type of life that the Grand Duke was ready to offer her.

'Why should it concern me?' he asked himself yet again.

Yet, as he moved around the Reception room, meeting old friends, being introduced by Katharina to some of the most prestigious personages in the Czar's entourage, he knew that he was only giving them half his attention.

In fact he was not doing his duty of probing deeply into what they were thinking about the War and the consequences of Bonaparte's invasion.

When the Czar and Czarina left, the rest of the guests followed and the Duke realised that, if he was to be changed in time for dinner in the Imperial apartments, he would have to hurry to his own room.

Katharina tightened her fingers on his as he raised her hand to his lips.

"Retire early this evening," she whispered, "I wish to talk to you."

"Talk?" the Duke queried.

"That is for you to decide," she replied softly.

There was no mistaking the invitation in her eyes or the fire he saw deep down in the dark depths of them.

'That is what I want,' he told himself as he walked away down the long corridor.

Yet by the time he had reached his own bedroom he was thinking not of Katharina but of Zoia.

Once again he was finding it just incredible that he should have felt what he had and experienced what amounted to a vision not once but twice in her presence.

Half-dressed the Duke moved to the window to look again at the last rays of the setting sun shimmering on the moving water of the River Neva.

'It's all the fault of this damned atmosphere!' he told himself and then added as many Russians had done before him,

'Why the devil could not Peter the Great have built this City with a better climate in another part of the country?'

He stood staring at the water, thinking what it must be like when it was frozen in the winter and the sky and the City of Palaces would seem frozen too.

'*The Ice Maiden!*'

Would she too melt with the spring that she had made him see when she played him the music that her father had written?

He found himself thinking about the figure that had come towards him through the trees and then he shied away from admitting who it had been.

He turned around and his valet was waiting for him, holding out his evening coat in his hands.

The Duke shrugged himself into it.

Made by Weston, the tailor patronised by the Prince Regent, it fitted without a wrinkle and he had already seen the Czar look at his coats speculatively and with an undoubted touch of envy in his eyes.

The valet added his decorations, taking them from velvet-lined boxes and fixing them in the correct places on his chest.

The Duke took a quick glance at himself in the mirror, an elaborately gilded one that had come originally from France and was, he knew, unique in both its age and its artistry.

Then, as the clock on the mantelpiece warned him that he only had a short time to reach the Czar's apartments, he set off down the corridors that seemed every time he traversed them to grow longer and longer.

It was the custom for each Czar to occupy a different part of The Winter Palace from his predecessors and Alexander had chosen for himself one that in many ways echoed his taste for simplicity.

The first Romanov to dispense with Royal pomp, he wore no jewellery and refused to allow people to dismount when they met him on the quay.

He liked to wander among his guests and had patterned his behaviour on that of an ordinary gentleman, using phrases as, 'I beg to be excused' and 'please do me the honour'.

Unfortunately in Russian eyes this diminished rather than increased the respect they had for him.

The Duke was fond of him and always had been because he believed that he was trying to rule in a different way from his mad father and the autocratic Catherine the Great.

It was, as he knew, no easy task to change anything in the Russian hierarchy, which, in the Palaces, ruled far more effectively than the Czar himself.

But the Duke had read reports from the British Ambassador about the incredible poverty and suffering in Russia and he knew that in the over-large perfumed rooms of The Winter Palace he was not seeing the real Russia that lay outside.

The reports spoke of filthy cellars not far from the Palaces where men and women were huddled together on wooden benches or on bundles of rags on the slimy wet ground.

"There are sixty, eighty, a hundred thousand, who have not enough to eat. There is not a face that is not bleared, blotched and blurred by drink. Dressed in rags most of them with bruised faces too sunken to speak, intent only to stay alive and not be put into the ice-cold ground. They are the dregs of the nation of eighty million and nothing can be done for them and nobody is in the least interested."

The Duke suddenly felt constrained and stifled.

He could not explain to himself why he had a sudden desire to be free of the Society he had come from London to seek and that in many ways was more polished and more appealing than he had expected.

'I must get away,' he told himself and was surprised at the urgency of his own feelings.

*

Tania burst into Zoia's bedroom where she was sitting mending the lace on one of her gowns which had been torn.

"Mama is taking me to call on some of her friends," she said. "I asked if you could come, but she wants to take me alone."

"But of course," Zoia answered. "And I will be here when you return."

"But I wanted you with us," Tania pouted. "It is so much more fun when afterwards we can talk over the people we have met and what they have said."

"If your mother wishes you to go with her alone," Zoia said, "there is nothing you can do about it and you can store up everything you have seen and heard to tell me about. And that will be exciting."

"It is not so exciting for me," Tania complained. "I cannot think why Mama is being so tiresome. She knows how happy we are together."

"Three women without a man to accompany them is an embarrassment to any hostess," Zoia smiled. "Go and enjoy yourself, dearest, and, when you come back, we will plan a new ballet dance to give your mother a surprise with."

"I would much rather dance with the handsome English Duke who was here yesterday," Tania said. "Mama has been talking about him to me and she says he has a delightful brother he particularly wants me to meet and that will be something to look forward to when we go to England."

Zoia noticed the word 'we' but she said nothing. She only tidied Tania's hair under her high crowned bonnet and then kissed her gently.

"Don't keep your Mama waiting," she urged. "You look very pretty and I am sure that there will be plenty of people to tell you so."

"I do wish you were coming," Tania repeated.

She hurried away leaving the door open behind her.

Zoia rose to close it, then changed her mind and, putting away the lace she had been mending, she went downstairs.

Now that there would be nobody in the house, it was an opportunity for her to play the piano and try out the new music that had arrived early today from Moscow.

Her father had sent it to her with a letter which told her what a success the orchestra had been at a performance the previous night and he had added,

> "There are rumours, scaremongers and a certain amount of quite needless panic. I am glad you are safe in St. Petersburg. At the same time you will know how much I miss you and how I shall look forward to when we can be together again. Don't worry about anything but enjoying yourself. I love you, my dearest daughter, and every time I play our special music, I know, we are very close."

Zoia had read the letter again and again.

There was no one like her father, she thought, who could say things that were exactly what one wanted to hear and which made the heart contract with joy.

It was true that, when they played certain music, they were close in way that brought Zoia an intense happiness.

She felt that it compensated her father a little for the loss of the wife he had loved with a devotion that had never wavered since the moment they had run away together.

'That is the sort of love I would hope to find one day,' Zoia told herself.

Because she had lived with such an example of married happiness she had known that she would never be content with a love that was not the highest and the best and which came from a man who was intrinsically a part of herself as she was a part of him.

It was difficult to put into words what she felt, but she could say it with music.

Just as many of her father's compositions were written in an effort to express the love he felt for his wife, so the music she played to herself when she was alone portrayed her own search for what was beautiful and Holy when it came to an expression of love.

From the moment her father had gone to Moscow two years ago, there had been men, who, having once seen her, had made every effort to make her acquaintance and court her.

It was then that her mother had explained to her, in more detail than she had ever done before, her exact position in life.

Zoia had always known that her mother's family, the Strovolskys, were one of the most important in Russia.

Her mother said frankly that she had committed an almost unforgivable crime in running away with the French Tutor, who had been employed to teach her and her brothers and sister to speak French.

"The aristocratic families like those in every country," the Princess Natasha had said, "do not connect marriage with love or love with marriage."

Zoia had listened wide-eyed as she went on,

"I knew that my grandfather was making every effort to find me a husband who would be condescending enough to overlook the fact that my father was Count Orlov, who did not marry my mother and accept me as a wife simply because I have Strovolsky blood in my veins."

The Princess's voice had sharpened as she added,

"It was not enough! Something within me rebelled at the thought of being condescended to and accepted under sufferance."

"I can understand that, Mama."

"I wanted love," the Princess Natasha said softly. "I wanted real love, the love that my mother, rightly or wrongly, had given Count Orlov and that she could never give to any other man."

She put her arm round her daughter.

"One day, my darling, you may have to face the same situation as I did. Then I promise you that love, real love, such as I have for your father, is worth all the sacrifices that one may have to make for it and nothing, I repeat nothing, else is of any consequence."

When Zoia saw the agony her father suffered when her mother died, she had known that, while she was watching his crucifixion at losing love, it was still the only thing worth having in the whole world.

She realised too that her mother's death had brought a new dimension to her father's music.

There was a depth in his compositions that had not been there before and he raised the playing of the orchestras he conducted to heights that they had never achieved previously.

'That is what love does,' Zoia told herself. 'It enlarges the capabilities and broadens the horizons of those who are able to find it.'

As she went downstairs, she heard below her the Princess and Tania leaving The Palace.

She had no intention of telling Tania so, but she understood exactly why the Princess did not wish to take her calling on her friends.

It was not only because she was slightly embarrassed by the fact that Zoia's father was only a musician and a Frenchman at that, it was also because only after they left Moscow had the Princess realised that despite Tania's beauty she was overshadowed by her friend.

Doting parents are proverbially blind and Zoia was sure, when the Princess had extended the generous invitation for her to accompany them to St. Petersburg, she had not expected that she would impinge on Tania's success in the Social world.

Zoia had no wish to go to St. Petersburg and leave her father, but then Pierre Vallon had insisted that she should do so.

"The Grand Duke is becoming more of a nuisance every day," he said bluntly, "and, when I am not with you, my dearest, I worry as to whether he will find some new way of forcing himself upon you. I find my anxiety interferes not only with my peace of mind but also with my work."

"Perhaps he will – follow me to – St. Petersburg?" Zoia suggested hesitatingly.

"He may certainly try," Pierre Vallon agreed, "but the Princess will deal with him more effectively than I can."

Zoia knew exactly what he meant.

It was difficult, even for such a distinguished man as her father, to stand up to and offend anyone of such importance as the Grand Duke Boris.

But the Princess Ysevolsov could speak to him on equal terms and Zoia knew that she would certainly not allow him to behave licentiously in any way while she was with Tania.

Because her father was so insistent and because secretly Zoia was rather frightened of the Grand Duke, she had finally agreed to go to St. Petersburg with the Princess and the huge retinue of servants who travelled with them.

They had left Moscow in no less than eighteen carriages and, although the journey had been tiring, Zoia had found herself interested in the countryside they were passing through, although sometimes the poverty of the peasants made her want to cry.

The journey had taken quite a long time for the simple reason that they had stayed with the Princess's friends en route.

It was then that the Princess had become aware of Zoia's attractions and wished that she had not been so hasty in extending her an invitation to stay with them at their Palace in St. Petersburg.

It was the Grand Duke Boris who had christened Zoia the *Ice Maiden* and the name had already preceded her so that everywhere they had stayed the men in the party eyed her with interest and wondered if perhaps they would be fortunate enough to melt the ice.

The Princess was made furious by their attentions.

She so wanted everybody to concentrate on her daughter and, although she had already planned that Tania should make a brilliant marriage, she thought that learning how to handle men, flattering them and certainly refusing their suit, would be an experience that should not be missed.

By the time they reached the second house on their route, it was obvious that the focus of attention was not Tania but Zoia and the Princess made her plans accordingly.

Zoia, she told herself, should take her rightful place when they reached St. Petersburg as companion and Teacher to Tania.

There would be no question then of her appearing in public or accepting invitations to parties.

She did not wish to be unkind and Sonya Ysevolsov was in fact a warm-hearted woman and made few enemies.

But she was prepared to fight fiercely and tenaciously for the well-being of her child and she was determined that Tania should make the most brilliant marriage that any girl had ever achieved.

This, in the Princess's eyes, meant marrying outside Russia.

She had seen much too much of the decadence and licentiousness of Society under the Romanovs and it was quite impossible to find anyone amongst her husband's relations or contemporaries who was happy.

Even the Czar with all his high-flown ideals, which had made so many people think that on his succession a new era was dawning, had early in his reign fallen deeply in love.

Madame Naryshkina was a lovely and dashing Polish lady who bore him two children and tormented him with her infidelities.

Because he was so much more of a gentleman than his predecessors, the Czar took great pains to pay public deference to his wife and they were acclaimed everywhere as the most handsome couple in Europe.

But it was not easy to say that the Czar, or for that matter the Czarina, were happy and the Princess longed for Tania not only to be of great social standing but to find happiness.

Englishmen, she had always believed, were excellent husbands.

They might have little moments of infidelity, *affaires de coeur* that were conducted with great propriety and discretion, but on the whole they appeared faithful and happy with their wives and their children.

It had therefore seemed providential to the Princess when she learned that the Duke of Welminster was coming to St. Petersburg as the Czar's guest.

She had not actually had an affair with the Duke herself, but she had flirted with him and thought him extremely fascinating when they had met both in London and Vienna.

'He is the type of man I have always admired,' the Princess had told herself.

She knew that the Duke found her as attractive as she found him and it was hard to resist the temptation of taking him as a lover.

But it would be far more of a triumph, she told herself, to have him as a son-in-law and, although he had made it clear that he wished to remain a bachelor, more obstinate men than he had changed their minds on that score.

And while she kept the Duke's brother in reserve, she had not quite given up hope where he himself was concerned.

As they drove away from The Palace, she started again to talk to Tania about the Duke's position in England, of his magnificent houses and fine possessions and of the very alluring qualities she found in him personally.

*

As it happened, Zoia, as she went downstairs, was also thinking about the Duke.

She had been conscious of his presence at the back of the box while she danced and she thought afterwards that it was strange she should notice that he was there.

When she concentrated on her father's music, she was usually carried away completely and lost in the world that he created for her so that she was oblivious of everything else.

And yet somehow at the back of her mind, hardly impinging on her consciousness but definitely there, she had known that there was a man standing at the back of the box.

When she had made her curtsey, she had seen him clearly behind the Princess, who was apparently unaware of his presence.

Then, as she came into the White Salon, she had been aware of him in a manner that seemed still a part of the music that her father had composed.

It was not what she felt about people ordinarily, it was something different, odd, yet in a way not odd, only familiar.

It was like a melody that she listened to with her heart as well as with her mind and that conjured up within her the desire to create.

That was what she felt she was doing when she danced nothing set or nothing that had been taught her, merely that which came from within herself.

Her father had always understood so well what she felt.

"When I compose, my dearest," he had said, "I feel sometimes as if I have opened a door within me and let the music come in. Then I only have to listen and it requires no other effort on my part."

"I listen too, Papa," Zoia had added. "And then I know what to do."

They had smiled at each other, knowing that there was no need for words to explain what happened because they understood.

'The Duke understands too,' Zoia thought as she reached the piano.

She sat down and played a few bars of her father's composition that she had played to him.

Then suddenly, as her father had said, the door within herself opened and she began to play something very different, something she heard in her heart and something that flowed through her and into her fingers so that she could interpret it into music.

She played and, as she did so, she saw the Duke, his eyes looking into hers when they had met. Then she saw the expression on his face when she had finished playing to him.

She had known in that second that he had understood what she was trying to convey and had seen what she had seen.

'How is it possible?' she asked.

And yet there was no question that it was indeed possible and that it had happened.

She played on and suddenly it was no surprise, but somehow inevitable that, as her music filled the room, he should come into it and walk towards her.

She glanced at him and went on playing and he stepped onto the dais and leaned on the piano as he had done the day before.

Only after two deep chords when she lifted her hands from the keys did the Duke say,

"I knew that I should find you here alone."

She looked up at him, her eyes on his.

"How – did you know – that?"

"I learnt last night that the Princess and her daughter would call at The Winter Palace this afternoon and I had a distinct feeling that you would not be included."

There seemed to be no answer to this and Zoia was silent.

"I may be wrong," the Duke went on, "but, when I came up the stairs and heard what you were playing, I had the strangest feeling that you were thinking of me."

Once again Zoia's eyes were on his and she replied softly,

"I – was thinking of you – just as I felt yesterday that when I – played what Papa had composed you – understood."

"I did," the Duke answered. "I fought against it, but I did understand."

There was silence and then he asked her,

"Did you compose what you were playing just now."

"I heard it for the – first time when I was – thinking of you."

The Duke drew in his breath.

There was a simplicity in the admission that robbed it of everything but the truth and yet because it was the truth it was all the more poignant.

"What have you done to me, Zoia?" he asked. "I have never felt like this in my life before."

"L-like – what?" she asked beneath her breath.

"Seeing things – hearing things. Being mystic, or any other word you may like to call it. It is completely foreign to my nature."

"How can you be so – sure of that?" Zoia asked. "And if it was – you would not have understood as you did – understand yesterday."

"Why should it happen?" the Duke enquired almost harshly. "Is it something to do with Russia or would this have occurred if we had been elsewhere, in London or Paris?"

Zoia looked down at the keyboard before she answered,

"I think – when things happen to us – as you are trying to say – it is because we are – ready for it. We may hear the same music – look at the same picture – see the same lovely view and it can mean nothing. And then suddenly – "

Her voice ceased as if she could find no more words and the Duke finished,

" – suddenly there is something else, a vision that I was convinced was only imagination until I came here today."

Zoia waited and he went on,

"The moment I saw you again I knew that it had been real. That is why I am asking, what have you done to me? Why should I feel like this?"

She gave him a smile that was the most beautiful smile that he had ever seen.

"It has – happened," she murmured, "and explanations are – quite unnecessary."

"But, of course, I am curious. Has this happened with other men?"

There was a sharpness in his voice as if he half-suspected that she was using hypnotism or some such other means of creating an effect.

Having asked the question, he waited, knowing that her reply was of importance out of all proportion to what it should have been.

"Only with Papa," Zoia answered. "He understands – he and I feel the same – but with no one else."

The Duke felt himself relax.

He had been afraid of what she might tell him.

"Shall we talk about it?" he asked, "or will you play to me?"

"Which would you prefer?"

"Both," he replied with a smile.

He leaned against the piano while Zoia lifted her hands and then looked down at them. And unexpectedly she dropped them back into her lap.

"Y-you are – making me shy," she said. "I-I cannot think of the music – because you are here."

"In other words you are thinking of me," the Duke responded in his deep voice.

"You – you want me to – play to you."

"Let it wait. Come and sit down on the sofa and tell me about yourself."

He straightened himself ready to move away from the piano.

For a moment Zoia did not rise.

"I think that Her – Highness would be annoyed if she knew that you – came here when she was – out," she stated slowly, as if she had just thought of it, "and we are – alone."

"Does it matter" the Duke asked. "Perhaps she will not know."

"She will know," Zoia answered, "because the servants will tell her. Everything is – known in Russia."

That was true, the Duke thought, just as Katharina had known yesterday that he had left The Winter Palace to visit the Princess.

He told himself that it was not important and he could not care what she said or thought.

Then he remembered that it concerned Zoia too and for the first time he realised that, in his desire to see her again, he had been incredibly selfish.

The Duke was so used to thinking only of his own interests and his own pleasures that he never considered how they might affect other people.

For the very first time in many years he found himself concerned with the effect of his actions on another human being and most especially on the girl facing him.

"I suppose the correct thing for me to do would be to leave at once," he suggested.

He looked at her and went on,

"I want to stay, God knows I want to stay! There is so much I want to talk to you about and so much I want you to tell me. But in case it should hurt you in any way, in case there should be unfortunate repercussions, I will give you a message for the Princess and leave."

Zoia clasped her hands together and it was an instinctive little gesture that made the Duke draw in his breath.

"I want you to – stay," she stammered in a low voice. "I should so much like to – talk to you – but I suppose it would be correct for me to ask you – to go."

"Let us compromise," the Duke proposed quickly. "I will stay a little longer, but we must not waste one second of our time together."

He put out his hand over the piano towards her.

"Come. Let us sit down comfortably and make the most of our time alone."

She rose and, as she did so, she put her hand in his.

As they touched each other, they were both aware of the vibrations that passed between them that were inescapable and compelling.

They had been about to step down from the dais, but now neither of them moved.

Zoia only raised her eyes, looked into the Duke's and for a moment time stood still.

"That is what I might have expected," he muttered.

His voice broke the spell.

She took her hand from his and walked across the room to sit on the satin-covered sofa that stood between two marble pillars.

He found himself watching the grace that she moved with and it was almost as if she floated rather than walked and there was music in every movement.

He sat himself down beside her, turning so as to look at her and searching her face.

"I heard a great deal about you last night," he started when she did not speak. "They tell me that you are called the *Ice Maiden.*"

Her eyes dropped a little shyly and a faint touch of colour came into her cheeks.

"It is – a foolish name thought up by a – foolish person."

"Why should you say that?" the Duke asked.

"Because I am not really – enclosed in ice," she answered, "except to one – particular person."

"The Grand Duke!"

"Yes – I don't like him and he attempts to – threaten Papa."

"In what way?" the Duke asked sharply.

"He told Papa that he would have him driven out of Russia and that he would not be allowed to conduct here, unless – unless I did as he – wished."

"That is intolerable!" the Duke reacted angrily. 'The Grand Duke has no right to behave in such an uncivilised manner."

"That is what – Papa said and he told the Grand Duke that he had no jurisdiction – over him. At the same time – I am afraid."

"Why?"

"The Grand Duke is a very obstinate and determined man. I have a feeling that he could also be – wicked and – unscrupulous if it suited him."

"You will be safe here in St. Petersburg."

"I – hope so," Zoia answered. "Her Highness is – very kind to me."

"I am sure she will protect you at any rate and, if you are in any trouble, I am also here."

Zoia looked at him and he had the feeling that she looked deep into his heart as if she was searching for something.

Then she said quietly,

"You must not be – involved in anything that might make – trouble for you with the Czar. I have heard how – fond he is of you – and Russian affairs should not concern you – personally."

The Duke smiled and answered.

"But you are not Russian, not entirely. You are half-French."

"That makes it worse! England is at war with France."

"So is Russia at the moment," the Duke added.

"I am very worried about Papa in Moscow. If the French reach it, the fighting will be – terrible."

"I feel certain that the Russians will do everything in their power to prevent the French from getting as far as Moscow," the Duke said slowly.

"It is all so – horrible – so unnecessary. I loved Paris when I was a little girl and we lived there – and it breaks Papa's heart to think of all the men who have been killed senselessly and for no reason – except for the insatiable ambition of one man who is not even French – but Corsican!"

It was a cry, the Duke thought, he had heard so many Frenchmen make and he had no answer to it.

Instead he said,

"I know I shall involve you in a great many difficulties if I stay here any longer, but I will see you again and, if you are really in any trouble, do *not* hesitate to let me know."

He paused and then he added,

"Promise me you will do so."

"I – promise," Zoia murmured softly.

He thought it was typical that she did not prevaricate and did not try to dramatise what he had said as so many other women might have done.

They both rose and the Duke took Zoia's hand in his.

She felt his lips on the softness of her skin.

"Take good care of yourself," he said quietly and walked away leaving the room without looking back.

She stood for a moment staring after him.

Then, as if she would still the tumult within her, her hands went to her breasts.

CHAPTER FOUR

Princess Ysevolsov and Tania called first on an ancient member of the Ysevolsov family, who lived in a fabulous Palace on the banks of the River Neva.

She was so old and had lived through so many dramatic events in her life that she was not particularly interested in what was happening at present.

She was, however, a tremendous admirer of the Czar and talked incessantly of his charm and his commanding appearance.

She had recently been visited by Madame de Staël, the French writer who had extolled him to all and sundry, saying that she was deeply affected by the noble simplicity with which he entered upon the great interests of Europe.

"Alexander," the old lady went on, "is exactly the type of Czar that the Russians have wanted for many centuries and you will see that history will grant him the place he deserves."

Tania found the visit to be rather boring, but contented herself with admiring the many attractive *objets d'art* that The Palace possessed.

When they left her, mother told her,

"At least one person is satisfied with the way that Russia is being ruled, but I cannot help feeling that such praise of his Imperial Majesty is exceptional."

"I think everybody admires the Czar, Mama," Tania answered. "He is so handsome and looks so commanding in his uniform."

The Princess bit back the rather bitter words that came to her lips and instead started to talk once again of the Duke.

"You must show him every attention, Tania. Smile at him and ask his opinion but, above all things, don't bore him with commonplace observations."

"What are they, Mama?"

The Princess, looking at her daughter, admitted to herself that, while Tania was indeed exceedingly lovely, her brains were not likely to entertain such a sophisticated gentleman as the Duke.

Their next call was at The Winter Palace where they enquired if it was possible to have an audience with the Czarina.

Elizabeth Feodorovna had always been extremely fond of the Princess and it was not surprising when the message came back that she would be delighted to see her.

The Princess and Tania were led to her private apartments and here again Tania was beguiled by all the attractive little ornaments in the private rooms.

The Czarina was, however, talking very seriously to the Princess.

She was, owing to the crisis, happier with the Czar than she had been for some time.

He no longer frittered away the hours with Maria Naryshkina. Instead he looked for the support of his wife, which she gave him wholeheartedly.

The Princess thought that the Czarina remained magnificently resolute.

"You are very courageous, ma'am," she declared.

"I try to be," the Czarina replied simply, "but how can I tell you of my inner emotions when my dear and well-beloved Russia, for whom I feel at this hour as for a darling child, is wretchedly sick?"

She gave a deep sigh and went on,

"I am certain that God will not abandon her, but she will suffer and I with her, sharing every spasm of her anguish."

The Princess put out her hand to press the Czarina's and make her understand how much she sympathised in her suffering.

Then in a quiet voice the Czarina went on to talk of her fund for war orphans and how she herself had handed over nine-tenths of her annual allowance to worthy charities.

It was growing late in the afternoon and the Princess was thinking that the Czarina would indicate that their interview was at an end when the door burst open and one of the Ladies-in-Waiting came rushing in with a distraught look on her face.

"Your Majesty, ma'am!" she cried.

The Empress rose to her feet, an apprehensive expression on her face as she asked,

"What is wrong? What has happened?"

"They are saying, ma'am," the Lady-in-Waiting answered almost incoherently, "that the French are starting a diversion in the direction of St. Petersburg."

"It cannot be true!" the Czarina exclaimed.

"I was told this by the Captain of the Golden Guard, ma'am, who had been informed that the Government are planning the evacuation of valuables."

"I just don't believe it!" the Czarina cried. "I must go to His Imperial Majesty at once!"

She went from the room and the Princess, taking Tania by the hand, started to make her way to the entrance of The Winter Palace.

The corridors were already full of people running hither and thither, talking at the tops of their voices and yet saying little that made any sense.

There were Chevalier Guards in gilt breastplates, Bishops wearing the white *klobouk* or high white veils falling from the crown of their hats to their shoulders and Court Arabs who were actually gigantic black men in *skorohods*.

The Princess bumped into a friend and she cried out,

"It is intolerable and inconceivable that we should be threatened here! Surely someone will stop the enemy before they reach us?"

"I am quite sure that is what will happen," the Princess said soothingly.

"I swear that I would tear out my tongue rather than speak the French language again!" her friend screamed hysterically, "and every Frenchman and woman in St. Petersburg should be expelled from the City immediately or sent to Siberia!"

She spat out the words venomously and then seemed to be swept away down the corridor by other people running, shouting and yelling out vehemently against the French and their leader, Napoleon Bonaparte.

The Princess found her carriage waiting and, as she and Tania drove away, the girl said tentatively,

"Will the French kill us, Mama?"

"I am sure that your father and the Russian Army will stop them long before they reach St. Petersburg," the Princess asserted firmly.

At the same time she crossed herself as she spoke and murmured a short prayer to God beneath her breath.

Back at the Ysevolsov Palace everything seemed to be calm and quiet after the tumult of The Winter Palace.

It was obvious that the bad news had not yet reached the servants and the Major Domo merely stepped forward to report,

"His Grace the Duke of Welminster called when you were out, Your Highness."

The Princess frowned.

"Did you tell him at what time I would return?"

"He did not ask, Your Highness, but he spoke for some time with Mademoiselle Vallon and she may have conveyed the information to him."

"He spoke with Mademoiselle Vallon?" the Princess asked sharply.

"He asked for her, Your Highness, and I informed His Grace that she was in the Music Room."

The Princess's lips tightened.

She had thought several times about the strange way that the Duke and Zoia had stood staring at each other when they had first met.

It had seemed peculiar at the time and now, as she remembered how interested the Duke had seemed in Zoia, her eyes darkened.

Without saying anything to Tania, she swept up the stairs and heard before she reached the landing, the sounds of music, which told her where Zoia was to be found.

She opened the door.

Zoia was sitting at the piano, her face raised, her eyes lifted as if she was looking into space and was totally unaware of what was happening in the world around her.

She had a radiant expression, which made her look lovelier than the Princess had ever seen her.

Harshly she banged the door behind her, shutting out Tania who had followed her mother upstairs.

The sound immediately jerked Zoia back to reality.

She ceased playing and rose slowly to her feet as the Princess advanced towards her.

When she reached the piano, the Princess demanded in a hard voice,

"I understand the Duke of Welminster has been here?"

"Yes, ma'am."

"And he stayed some time?"

"Not for – very long, ma'am."

"How long?"

"I don't know exactly," Zoia replied.

"You know as well as I do, you have no right to entertain gentlemen in my absence. It is not the way I expect a young woman staying in my house to behave."

"I am sorry, ma'am," Zoia answered, "but the Duke came into the room unexpectedly. When he realised that you were not at home – he talked for a few minutes and then left."

"What did he say? What did he talk about?"

Zoia was quiet for a moment and then she answered,

"About music – and my father."

Because she appeared to answer the question in such a straightforward and truthful way, the Princess should have been placated, but somehow it seemed to make her angrier than she was already.

All the resentment she felt at Zoia overshadowing Tania and the way, without apparently making any effort she attracted men, seemed to boil up inside her until she could no longer contain herself.

"Your countrymen are marching on St. Petersburg," she snapped. "They threaten our lives and everything we hold dear and sacred. You had best return to your father for I have no intention of sheltering an enemy!"

As the Princess had begun to speak, Zoia's eyes widened and there was no doubt of her astonishment at what she heard.

Then, as the Princess finished, almost spitting the last words at her, she said quietly but with a dignity that was unassailable,

"I understand, ma'am, and I will leave immediately – for Moscow. I can only thank you for your hospitality and say that my father and I are – very grateful."

She curtseyed and, as if the Princess was suddenly aware of how young and slight she was, she said in a voice that was a little less aggressive,

"I will order a travelling carriage for you and enough of our most trusted servants to accompany you and ensure your safety."

"Thank you – very much, ma'am."

Zoia curtseyed again and went from the room.

*

The Duke was with the Czar when the rumour that Napoleon was now moving towards St. Petersburg was brought to him.

Alexander read the despatch and his face paled as he handed it without saying a word to the Duke.

The Duke read what was written in large sprawling and half-unintelligible writing in the communiqué and commented,

"Quite frankly, I don't believe this, Sire."

"Why not?" the Czar enquired.

"Because if it was true you would have heard from General Kutuzov himself."

"The despatch is not from him?"

"No, Sire. It has been sent to you by Count Povolsk who, I think you will remember, was in your suite when we met in Vienna."

"Yes, yes, I do remember."

"I always thought the Count to be a dilettante and a gossiper. I don't know what position he holds in the Russian Army, but I would not rate it very high."

The Czar snatched the despatch from the Duke's hand and read it again.

"I believe you are right," he admitted. "We should not pay too much attention to this until we have further confirmation from Kutuzov himself."

Unfortunately when the Duke left the Czar's apartments, he found that the despatch had been read by Members of the Government before it reached the Czar and the Courier who carried it had conveyed its contents to everybody he met.

It was the kind of thing, he knew, that would never have happened in the British Army and he was appalled at the hysteria that had taken possession not only of The Winter Palace but also of the inhabitants of St. Petersburg.

He soon learned that the majority of the noble families were packing their valuables into carriages and moving from the City to their houses in the country.

So only the poor would be left helpless and unprotected and crowds of them now stood outside The Winter Palace, staring at the huge edifice as if they felt that only some Divine Providence linked with the Czar himself could save them.

The Duke was certain that with Moscow directly in their line of advance and far nearer it was extremely unlikely that Napoleon would change direction and march on St. Petersburg.

What he might do after capturing Moscow was a very different matter, but the Duke, who at one time had been a soldier himself, was quite certain from a Military point of view that St. Petersburg would not be the immediate objective.

It was, however, difficult to find anyone to discuss it with him let alone agree with him.

Finally he talked to Lord Cathcart, the British Ambassador, who informed him, what he had not known before, that Sir Robert Wilson, who was known as 'the English General', was with the Russian Army.

Sir Robert had acquired a European reputation as an expert on Russia at war when he had written a book published two years earlier and studied by all the Military specialists of the age including Napoleon Bonaparte himself.

Lord Cathcart informed the General that Sir Robert had been sent out by the British Government from Turkey to the Russian Front and had arrived only just in time to witness the fall of Smolensk.

"He is with them now," Lord Cathcart said, "and I am awaiting a report from him about what is occurring."

He smiled as he added,

"You will understand, Your Grace, that I find his reports very much more credible than those that come from the Russians and they often mislead the Czar."

The Duke then settled himself more comfortably in the chair in the Ambassador's very impressive Reception room.

"I am very relieved at what you tell me, my Lord," he said, "and, if it is true that you are expecting a despatch at any moment, I would like to wait for it."

"I shall be delighted for you to do so," Lord Cathcart replied.

The Courier, however, carrying the despatch from Sir Robert Wilson did not arrive until very late in the evening.

The Duke stayed on at the British Embassy for dinner and only when they had finished an excellent meal did a servant intimate to his host that the Courier had just arrived.

There was no doubt that both the Ambassador and the Duke were feeling tense as the Ambassador himself undid the despatch.

He read it first and then, with a sigh that was obviously one of relief, he passed it to the Duke.

Robert Wilson wrote crisply and positively that he understood General Kutuzov intended to halt his retreating troops who had been moving steadily back in front of the advancing French and would engage the invaders in battle before they reached Moscow.

"That is Bonaparte's current objective," he wrote *"And there is no doubt that he must be prevented from achieving it."*

That was the end of the despatch, which was a short one and the Duke looked at the Ambassador with a smile as he said,

"I was certain that the panic that has swept St. Petersburg was completely unnecessary."

"So was I," Lord Cathcart nodded.

He rose to his feet.

"1 must carry this immediately to the Czar, but I would be grateful, Your Grace, if you would be kind enough to inform any Members of the Government who are available what we have just learned."

"I will," the Duke agreed.

It was, as it happened, no easy task. However, nearly three hours later, the Duke knew that he and the Ambassador between them had arranged for a great number of panic-stricken orders to be countermanded and prevented a number of people of influence from leaving the City.

By this time the Duke was very tired and, when finally he retired to his bedroom, he hoped that tonight Katharina would not be demanding his attention.

He had not really had time during the day to think about what his reaction last night had been when she had come to him as before through the secret panel in the wall.

He had known, as she advanced towards him wearing a new and even more attractive *negligée* than she had worn the night before, that his interest in her had died and, incredible though it seemed, she no longer attracted him.

He had not for one moment assumed that their interest in each other was anything but a passionate exchange between two sophisticated people who really appreciated the expertise of making love.

That physically she was eminently desirable went without saying and the Duke without conceit knew that she did not exaggerate when she described him as an exceptional lover.

She amused and aroused him in equal proportions.

What was more his knowledge that she was there to spy on him gave a piquancy to their affair which he appreciated as she did.

Then, quite unexpectedly, almost like a bombshell, he knew that his feelings for her had changed and, even if he wished to do so, he could no longer play the role of her lover.

Because he was half-prepared for his reaction to what she expected of him, he had not undressed.

His valet had taken away his evening coat with its decorations and he had loosened his tightly tied cravat, but, when she appeared, he was still wearing his fine lawn shirt and black satin knee-breeches with the diamond garter glittering against his black silk stockings.

Before Katharina could speak and before she could ask him the obvious question as to why he was not in bed, the Duke said rapidly,

"I have some urgent despatches to write, Katharina, and they will keep me busy until the early hours of the morning.".

She smiled.

"Then I will write them with you. You know how I wish to read them."

"Unfortunately they will be in code and, although your countrymen have attempted to break it, I don't think as yet they have managed to do so."

"That is true and all the more reason, my adorable Blake, for you to translate them to me."

"Can you really imagine me committing such treachery?" the Duke questioned. "I have not asked you to show me *your* confidential reports."

"You may see them if you wish," Katharina replied, "but I can tell you far more easily what I think about you and what you are like as a *man*."

The last word was a caress in the way she said it and the Duke answered swiftly,

"Go to bed, Katharina and leave me with my work."

"Can you really be so unkind?" she almost demanded.

She moved towards him and, before he could avoid it, her arms were round him and her lips were against his shoulder.

He could feel them warm and possessive through his thin shirt, but, as she touched him, he knew, as he had known when she came into the room, that she no longer had any power over him.

It was difficult to believe it because their liaison had been so fiery and their desire for each other almost a violent confrontation.

The Duke put his fingers under Katharina's small chin and turned her face up to his.

For a long moment he looked into her eyes and, seeing the fire lurking in their depths while her breath was coming quickly through her parted lips.

'How has this happened?' he asked himself and knew the answer as if somebody had called it aloud.

Only when Katharina had left him reluctantly and he was alone as he wished to be, did he walk to the window and pull back the curtains to breathe in the hot windless air.

As he did so, he heard in his mind the music that Zoia had played and that her father had called *The Melting of the Ice*.

He thought to himself as he listened that it melted within himself years of cynicism and of assuring himself that women fell into two categories only, those who were desirable and those who were not.

Tonight it was not any sort of physical barrier that had been erected between himself and Katharina but an idealistic one.

He felt as if he was a Knight entering a joust and, because he carried the favour of his lady, all other women had ceased to have any meaning for him.

It seemed utterly incredible and yet he knew that it had happened.

The music that Zoia played seemed to deepen and to encompass not only his mind but a part of his anatomy that he had not known for a very long time, but which he had once called his 'soul'.

*

When the Duke rose the next morning, he found that The Winter Palace had returned to normal and the confusion and chaos of the day before might never have materialised.

The Grenadiers of the Golden Guard were as impassive as statues as the Duke proceeded along the corridors to the Czar's apartment and the people he met, who were mostly officials, walked slowly and circumspectly passing him with a deep respectful bow as though they had never heard of the word 'panic'.

The Czar was in an excellent mood, certain from his Bible readings of the night before that Kutuzov would somehow, because he was favoured by God Himself, prevent the French Army from reaching Moscow.

As the Duke listened to him, an idea began gradually to present itself to his mind, but for the moment he did not voice it.

However, he left The Winter Palace as soon as he could excuse himself from attendance on the Czar and set off once again in the direction of the Ysevolsov Palace.

He told himself that it would be only polite to let Princess Ysevolsov of all people know that all the rumours, which she would most undoubtedly have heard, of Napoleon marching in the direction of St. Petersburg were totally untrue.

But he soon realised that his real motive for going to the Ysevolsov Palace was to see Zoia again.

All last night, when without bothering to write any despatches, he had climbed into bed, he first of all thought about her and then dreamt about her.

'She is beginning to haunt me,' he told himself and wondered once again if it was part of the mystery and climate of Russia or did the explanation lie in something that he would not yet admit frankly to himself?

At the Ysevolsov Palace he was pleased to see that there were no carriages being loaded up in the courtyard and, when he asked to see the Princess, he was taken immediately to her private sitting room.

As he was announced, the Princess, who was sitting at her secrétaire writing, gave a cry of delight and rose to her feet.

"Blake!" she exclaimed. "I am so delighted to see you and I am sure that you can answer many questions that I am longing to ask."

"I expect you have already heard," the Duke replied, "that the panic yesterday was only a rumour spread by that indefatigable scandalmonger Count Povolsk."

The Princess laughed.

"I might have guessed that Felix would be at the bottom of it, but fortunately one of my friends called late last night to say that he had seen Lord Cathcart and there was no need for any of us to become excited."

"I felt that you, if nobody else, would be sensible," the Duke remarked.

"I must order some refreshment," the Princess smiled. "Will you have coffee or wine?"

"Coffee, please," the Duke replied.

The Princess rang a gold bell and gave the order.

The Duke waited until the door closed behind the servant and then he said,

"I hope that Zoia Vallon was not upset by the rumour. I feel certain that she is already deeply concerned with the fate of her father in Moscow."

"Pierre Vallon is a Frenchman," the Princess said coldly, "and, after what we all felt last night, it will take quite some time before any of us regard the French as anything but our most implacable enemy!"

The Duke looked at her in surprise.

"Surely that does not include Vallon and his daughter?"

"I am afraid, Blake, when my husband is likely to be killed by a French bullet and his country invaded in this despicable manner, I have little use for French citizens whoever they may be."

The Duke was astonished but, because his concern was instantly for Zoia, he said to the Princess quickly,

"May I speak with Vallon's daughter? I feel that she must be extremely distressed by your attitude."

"There is no reason for you to concern yourself," the Princess replied. "After all she is nothing to you."

"I was extremely struck by her talent as a dancer and by the way she plays the piano."

He mentioned the piano deliberately, knowing full well that the servants would have told the Princess that he had been to the Music Room while she was playing.

"That I can well believe," the Princess answered, "but I suggest we talk of other things, for I have no intention, dear Blake, of quarrelling with you over an unimportant young girl who was merely teaching my daughter French."

"We certainly will not quarrel, but I would still like to speak to Zoia. I feel sure that you will not prevent me from doing so."

He saw the Princess's eyes narrow for a moment.

Then she exclaimed,

"So persistent! I must say, Blake, I am surprised at you. I never thought for a moment that a young girl would really interest you, but if so, why not my little Tania?"

"I have already said that I think that Tania would suit my brother admirably," the Duke replied patiently. "I will also, and this is a promise, give a ball for her at Welminster House when you bring her to London."

The Princess was well aware of what a concession this was and she clasped her hands together as she said,

"That is wonderful of you, Blake, and I know exactly what it will mean for Tania as an *entrée* to the *Beau Monde*."

She gave a little laugh and put her fingers to her lips.

"There, you see, I am talking French when everybody swore yesterday that never again would a French word pass their lips! But how else could one describe the glittering exclusive circle that you are such a prominent figure in?"

"You are very flattering, Sonya, but I still wish to speak to Zoia."

The Princess's eyes met his and he thought that she intended to defy him. Then, with a smile that had something slightly spiteful about it, she parried,

"Unfortunately that is impossible."

"Why?"

"Because Zoia left at dawn this morning for Moscow."

"You mean you sent her away?"

"I sent her back to her father."

"Why?"

"Because she is French and I thought that she would be safer there when feelings here against the French are running so high."

"You really thought that Moscow, which at any moment will be within the reach of Napoleon's guns, is safer?"

The Duke spoke scathingly and the Princess looked at him a little apprehensively before she said,

"It is none of your business, Blake, what I do in my own household or with someone who is more or less a superior servant."

The Duke rose to his feet

"You are leaving?" the Princess asked and now there was a note of consternation in her voice.

"I am leaving," the Duke replied. "Goodbye, Sonya."

He raised her hand perfunctorily to his lips, bowed and left the room.

"Blake!" she called out in a pleading tone just before the door closed behind him, but he did not appear to hear her.

The Duke returned to The Winter Palace, gave orders to his valet to pack his suitcases immediately and then went to the Czar's apartments.

Alexander was engaged with a number of Statesmen, but as soon as he was free the Duke was admitted to his presence.

"What is it, Welminster?" he enquired. "I have a feeling that you would not have asked to see me urgently unless it was important."

"It is important to me, Sire. I have decided that, after the commotion and confusion of last night, I should in the interests of my own country and perhaps of yours, go immediately to try to make contact with Sir Robert Wilson."

"You would liaise with my Army?"

"I should like to have the pleasure of meeting General Kutuzov," the Duke replied, "and to be able to see for myself exactly what is taking place. I think after last night, Sire, that we would both of us be rather sceptical of despatches from whichever direction they come."

"The Government behaved with quite unseemly haste," the Czar said sharply. "I have already spoken to them sternly and telling them that in the future they must make sure of their facts."

"You are quite right to do so, Sire," the Duke agreed, "and, if you will not think it is an impertinence, I should like to send you my own observations on what is occurring when I am in touch with Kutuzov."

"Please do that. You know that I trust you, Welminster, and I shall always be grateful for your help yesterday evening."

There was no need for the Czar to express in words that he was very ashamed that he, his Government and a large number of other prominent Russians had panicked with very little reason for it.

Leaving the Imperial apartments, the Duke hurried to his own and found, as he expected, that everything was ready for him to leave at once.

He wrote a hurried note to the British Ambassador and, because he felt that it was the decent thing to do, he wrote one also to Katharina.

Then, almost like a boy hurrying from school to go home for the holidays, he ran down the marble staircase and out to where a *drotski* was waiting for him with another for his valet and six mounted soldiers ordered by the Czar to be his escort.

As they drove away from The Winter Palace, the Duke felt as if he was setting out on a voyage of discovery.

Not as far as the War between the two Armies was concerned, but as regards himself, his feelings and perhaps, although he was not sure, his whole future.

*

The Ysevolsov travelling carriage drawn by four horses was very swift and Zoia already knew that Prince Ysevolsov, like many nobles, he had his own horses stabled at convenient stopping places between St. Petersburg and Moscow.

She thought that at the rate they were travelling she would be with her father within five to six days and knew that in some ways it would be a great relief to be with him again.

Yet he might be angry with her for coming into danger that included not only the threat from the French but from the Grand Duke Boris as well.

He had made life intolerable for her until her father persuaded her to leave Moscow.

Because he could not obtain entrance to the house to see her, he was permanently outside the door, preventing her from going out and making his presence known by a long stream of presents, bouquets of flowers and letters.

She refused to communicate with him and his gifts of any obvious value were returned immediately by the servants.

But it had given her the uncomfortable feeling of being besieged, and she was frightened all the time that the Grand Duke in frustration might take his revenge upon her father.

No Russian, whoever he might be, would dare to defy or offend anyone of the Grand Duke's importance.

But, as Pierre Vallon laughed at his threats and discounted his rudeness, Zoia trembled, knowing that there is an obstinacy and determination in the Russian character that would make a man fight and go on fighting even when he is beaten.

That was what Zoia prayed Napoleon Bonaparte would find as he invaded Russia, but so far he had been victorious and the Russians had been defeated in every engagement.

She could not help feeling that her sympathies were torn in two between the conflicting forces since she was half-French and half-Russian.

But she told herself that in this instance, if in none other, her sympathy was entirely with the land of her mother.

The French had no right, she thought, to invade another country that had done them no harm and had in fact for a short time been their ally.

She had learned that the Czar had sent a message to Bonaparte at Vilna, saying that it was not too late to maintain peace even now if the Emperor would take his Army back across the River Niemen.

"Even God could not now undo what has been started," Napoleon countered.

Zoia had been told that, when Alexander had received the reply, he remarked,

"At least Europe will now appreciate that we are not beginning this slaughter."

But whoever had begun or ended it, men on each side would die and to Zoia there was something terrible in thinking of the young men who would not only be shattered by the guns but also be wounded and left to ebb out their lives in agony as there was no one to attend to them.

'War is wrong and wicked,' she said to herself passionately and found herself praying that no one she loved should be either killed or wounded.

And somehow her prayer inevitably included the Duke.

She had known when he left her that he had taken some part of herself with him.

She had wanted him to stay, she had wanted, when she turned again to the piano to see him and hear his voice, to feel that strange vibration between them that seemed to strike into her very soul and somehow make her his captive.

Now that they had been parted and she felt as the horses carried her away on the road to Moscow that they would never meet again and probably he would soon have forgotten her very existence.

It was an inexpressible agony within her heart while she could not imagine it possible that this could have happened to her.

He had walked into her life so unexpectedly and yet in that second when their eyes met she had felt as if she had found him again after endless centuries of time.

She dared not attempt to understand what had happened to her. She only knew that it had and suddenly the music she heard within herself and which she could express with her fingers held a new meaning.

Even her prayers had changed and, when she thought about the Duke, her whole being seemed to come alive.

But she was leaving him behind in St. Petersburg and perhaps he would never know why she had left.

Perhaps it would be days before he even found out that she had gone.

Because this hurt her so, she felt as if her whole being winged through the ever-widening space between them to reach him.

And yet, she asked herself, how could she think for one moment that she could ever be of any importance in the Duke's life although already he meant so much to *her*?

She now understood exactly what her mother had said to her when she had explained exactly why she had run away with her father in spite of the grandness of her position in her grandfather's household, the grandeur they lived in and the distinction of being a Strovolsky.

It was all of no consequence beside love.

But her mother's position was very different, Zoia thought, from her own.

Her mother had loved a man who was considered to be her inferior, while she loved a man who was infinitely her superior in every way. He was a man of great authority and of a different nationality so that between them lay a gulf as wide as the distance from the earth to the moon.

'I must forget him,' Zoia whispered and she knew that it would be just impossible.

She would never forget him and she thought, perhaps because of what she had felt for him on the three brief occasions when they had met and he had filled her whole world that she would always be the *Ice Maiden* they declared her to be.

On and on the horses travelled. And they stopped for picnic meals that the servants had brought with them and for a change of horses.

They travelled both by day and by night because it would have been impossible for Zoia to stay alone at night in an inn.

What was more, she had always been told that they were scruffy, dirty and lice-ridden and doubtless at the moment filled with the Military.

So that those who escorted her could get some sleep, they often stopped for an hour or so by the road and the men who drove the carriages and rode as outriders merely dropped down on the ground, warm from the great heat of the sun, and slept without moving.

Then they would awaken refreshed and ready to ride on.

It was constricting, but Zoia grew used to the movement of the carriage beneath her and sometimes she felt as though she was on a long pilgrimage which there was no end to and the rumble of the wheels seemed to fill her ears to the exclusion even of thought.

Then, when they were coming to what she thought must be the end of their journey, there was the distant sound of gunfire.

She had seen the movement of Russian troops in increasing numbers and one of the servants told her that the peasants had said that the Russians were preparing to counterattack the French.

Zoia wondered where this would be. The night before, when they had stopped for a meal beneath some trees, she had asked the coachman where they were and he pointed to the South and answered,

"Borodino."

She had known, for she had heard of it before, that it was in the direction of Moscow and she thought with relief how wonderful it would be to see her father on the morrow.

She only hoped that he had not, by some frightening mischance, already left the City and she would find herself alone there without him.

But his letters had seemed so calm and unperturbed that she could not believe he would run away and certainly he would not move unless his orchestra went with him.

Now, as dawn broke, and they started on their way, she heard cannon again, far away to the South and realised that the battle everybody in St. Petersburg had been waiting for had begun.

Zoia felt almost as if she was being threatened by those on each side of the conflict, the Russians because she was French and the French because she was Russian.

She found herself praying for her own safety and somehow she found herself praying for the Duke's safety as well, although why he should be in any danger she had no idea for she was sure that he was still in St. Petersburg.

On and on the horses went and now at last there were the domes and spires of Moscow ahead.

'I am home!' Zoia told herself, for home was where her father was, although it could never be the same since her mother was no longer there too.

She was tired for it had been a long journey and, as she still heard the noise of cannon now far away in the distance, she thought that the men facing the firing must be tired too, although by now many of those on both sides would be dead.

She shivered at the thought, thinking once again that it was a cruel waste of the most precious gift God that had given to mankind – the gift of life.

Now they were in the City of Moscow and she could see that the streets were filled with people all obviously tense and waiting for the outcome of the battle.

The carriage drove along the riverside, past the Kremlin with its high pointed towers and then, some way further on, it turned up a street where there were well-built stone houses.

Her mother had always said that she had no wish to live in a house built of wood and, because Pierre Vallon loved his wife so much that he was always prepared to do anything that would make her happy, he had bought a house in a quiet square some way from the centre of the City and Natasha Vallon had been delighted with it.

"There is a garden where Zoia and I can sit under the trees," she enthused, "and where, when it is warm enough, you and I, my darling, will have our breakfast. It is like an adorable doll's house and we will be very happy here."

Pierre Vallon kissed his wife.

"You have never grown up," he laughed. "A doll's house is what I should give you in every country where we have to live."

His wife had looked at him in an adoring fashion.

"As long as it is a home that you will always return to," she said softly, "I would be happy in a garret or a cellar. It is of no consequence to me."

He put his arms around her and Zoia, who was watching, knew that he was moved by her mother's words in the same way that music moved him so that there was a look in his eyes which she could only describe to herself as one of rapture.

'The doll's house' as they called it teasingly had been an oasis of peace and happiness where Pierre Vallon could escape from everything, even from his admirers who pursued him relentlessly.

It was only the Grand Duke Boris who had upset the peace and quiet and Zoia had been more thankful than ever for the garden when she dared not leave her own front door for fear of encountering him.

Now for the moment there was no fear that the Grand Duke was lurking outside and, as the carriage drew to a standstill, she jumped out of it before her attendants had even time to knock on the door.

It was opened by her father's housekeeper who stared at her in surprise.

"M'mselle Zoia!" she exclaimed.

"I am back, Maria," Zoia answered. "Is Papa here?"

"He's in the garden, *m'mselle*," Maria replied and Zoia sped through the house.

Her father was sitting in the shade of a tree with sheets of music in front of him and she knew that he was writing down his latest composition for his orchestra to play.

She paused and stood for a moment gazing at him.

Could any man, she asked, be more handsome and more attractive?

Then her heart answered,

'Yes, there is one,' before with a little cry that startled Pierre Vallon, she ran underneath the branches of the trees.

"Papa, *Papa*! I am home!"

She saw the surprise in her father's eyes and then his arms went around her and he was holding her close.

"Zoia, my dearest. Why are you back here in Moscow? How could you do anything so crazy as to return at this dreadful moment?"

CHAPTER FIVE

"The troops are abandoning the City, sir," Jacques announced as he served luncheon to Zoia and her father.

"Nearly everybody else seems to have left already," Pierre Vallon replied.

Zoia looked at him in surprise and he explained,

"The Governor of the City has forbidden the people to leave and pleaded with them and brought them back and punished those he could catch, but they still continue to slip away with their carriages full of everything they can pack into them."

"I am sure that the Russian Army has stopped the French," Zoia pointed out. "I heard the guns in the distance soon after dawn. It must have been about six o'clock and I cannot bear to think of how many men will have been killed."

"One cannot have war without casualties," Pierre Vallon replied. "I can only pray that the battle has been decisive one way or another."

Even though he spoke as if it mattered little to him which side won, Zoia was quite sure that in his heart he resented it that his own countrymen were the aggressors.

'Napoleon has taken far too much already,' she thought. 'Why on earth should he want more? Why should he wish to master Russia as well as nearly the whole of Europe?'

"There's a new broadsheet, sir," Jacques said, bringing it from the side table where he had put it.

"What does it say?" Pierre Vallon asked without attempting to take it from him.

"It declares that General Kutuzov will defend Moscow to the last drop of his blood."

"That is what I suppose he is doing at this moment," Pierre Vallon remarked.

As he spoke, he was obviously listening and Zoia could also hear, very faintly for they were a long distance away, the thundering of cannon.

It seemed to her, although it was difficult to tell if it was a fact, that the firing was more intense and more explosive than when she had been near Borodino on the road approaching the City.

"We are safe – here?" she asked and there was just a tremor of fear in her voice.

"I imagine we will be safe, whichever side is victorious," her father replied dryly. "But I do wish, my dearest, you had stayed in St. Petersburg."

Because she thought that it would hurt him, Zoia had not told her father that the Princess had literally turned her out.

Instead she said,

"If there is danger I want to be with you, Papa, and I know that is where Mama would wish me to be."

Her father smiled at her and she could see the sadness in his eyes which was always there when he thought about his wife.

He rose from the table and walked to the window to look out into the sunlit garden.

"What we have to decide," he said, "is if it is best for us to stay or to leave."

"If we leave, where shall we go?" Zoia asked him.

"That, of course, is the problem. What do you think, Jacques?"

There was nothing unusual in Pierre Vallon discussing his plans with the man who was ostensibly their servant, although actually his position was a very different one.

Jacques had been an unsuccessful actor who had met Pierre Vallon by chance and had then dedicated his life to his service.

He had had a very unhappy childhood. He had wandered about in circuses taking part in minor turns and, although he had been given small parts on the stage from time to time, no one had been interested in him or wished to retain his services.

Then, by chance, when he was out of work, he went to the Opera and saw Pierre Vallon conducting.

From that moment, as he had told Zoia, he found his soul and knew that this was what he had been searching for all his life.

He had now been in their household for nearly ten years and it was difficult to imagine what life would be without him.

Apart from anything else Jacques had an aptitude for languages and he not only spoke German because he had once lived in Vienna and Arabic from visiting Egypt but now he was surprisingly proficient in Russian.

He could act the part he wished to play much more convincingly than he was able to do on the stage and Zoia recognised that, whoever occupied Moscow, Jacques would be able to converse with them and prove that he was a kindred spirit.

"I suppose it will be difficult to buy food if the shopkeepers have left and the – shops are closed," she asked aloud.

"I've got in a good store, *m'mselle*," Jacques answered.

She smiled because she knew that, whoever else went hungry, her father would not if Jacques had anything to do with it.

"One thing I must insist upon," Pierre Vallon said with a note of authority in his voice that Zoia had not heard before, "you are not, for any reason whatsoever, to leave the house."

"Do you mean that, Papa?" she asked, remembering how frustrated she had felt before she left Moscow because the Grand Duke's behaviour had forced her to remain a prisoner in her own home.

"I mean it," Pierre Vallon insisted firmly.

He looked at Jacques as he spoke and the two men were thinking that an almost empty City would be a temptation to the Russian soldiers, let alone the French, who had fought their way for so many weary miles from their homeland. Looting was always one of the 'perks' of war and both men were certain that there would be uncontrollable looting, just as a woman, any woman, would be a temptation to men separated from their wives and sweethearts.

"You are to stay in the house," Pierre Vallon repeated and, as if he did not wish to say anything more, he went from the room.

"You were unwise to come back, *m'mselle*," Jacques said to Zoia. "It'll worry the Master and he doesn't work so well when he's worried."

Zoia glanced over her shoulder at the closed door before she answered,

"I just had to come, Jacques, only don't tell Papa. People in St. Petersburg thought that Napoleon might be marching in that direction and suddenly everybody hated the French and the Princess wished to be rid of me."

Jacques shrugged his shoulders.

"*C'est la guerre, m'mselle*, and in war anything may happen."

As her father had done, Zoia went to the window.

She thought that she could hear the thunder of cannon although it was really too far away and she could imagine the sound of falling shells and the moans and cries of the wounded and the smell of blood and powder.

She had never seen a battle and yet she felt the horror of it instinctively and she turned away from the sunshine and moved into the small salon at the front of the house.

Then, very suddenly, at four o'clock in the afternoon, she sensed an abrupt silence and she knew without being told that the battle was over.

Now it was the question of who had won?

Zoia had a feeling of apprehension that was different to anything that she had felt all day. She did not understand why she was so tense and in a way afraid.

She ran from the salon in search of Jacques and found him polishing a piece of silver in the kitchen and said,

"I know that the guns have – ceased. The battle is now over! Oh, Jacques, please find out what has happened."

"The Master should be home soon," Jacques replied.

"He will be with the orchestra and I cannot wait until he returns. Please, Jacques, find out if anybody knows the result of the battle."

"I don't like leavin' the house with only two women in it," he said, "but to please you, *m'mselle*, I'll see what I can learn. Bolt the door after I've gone and don't open it to anyone except the Master or myself."

"No – of course not," Zoia agreed.

At the same time it made her feel strange to hear such instructions from Jacques.

She went to talk to Maria, but it was hard to keep her mind on anything but the battle and her anxiety to know what had occurred.

It was nearly two hours before Jacques returned. As soon as she heard his knock on the door, Zoia ran down the stairs and, peeping through a side window, saw him outside.

She pulled back the bolts, turned the key and he came into the small hall.

He was smiling and she knew before he spoke that he brought good news.

"What has – happened? What have you – learned?"

Her words fell over themselves.

"They say it's a great victory, *m'mselle*."

"For the Russians?"

"Of course! They always said that General Kutuzov would stop Napoleon from reaching Moscow."

"Then we need not worry anymore," Zoia cried in delight and ran upstairs to tell Maria the good news.

When her father came back to the house, he did not seem as pleased and excited as she had thought he would be.

"There have been terrible casualties," he related. "Some wounded are being brought into the City and there is practically nobody still here to attend to them."

"Surely everyone cannot have gone, Papa?"

"There are only the poor and homeless to be seen in the streets," Pierre Vallon replied, "and do you know how many of my orchestra came to the rehearsal that I had called for this afternoon?"

"How many?" Zoia asked.

"Six!" he replied.

He flung the music sheets he held in his hand down on the table as he asserted,

"The orchestra is finished! I am no longer wanted!"

"Oh – Papa."

Because Zoia felt the pain in his voice, she went to him and put her arms around him.

"You will always be wanted," she stressed reassuringly, "if not in Russia then in a dozen other countries. You know that only too well!"

"They were coming along so splendidly," Pierre Vallon said almost beneath his breath. "I felt because they were your mother's countrymen that they somehow kept me in touch with her."

He spoke more to himself than to his daughter and Zoia, pressing her cheek against his, said,

"Wherever you are I know Mama is always – with you. You were too close ever to lose –one another."

She felt her father's arms tighten round her and knew that was what he wanted to hear.

Then, as if he could not bear to talk anymore, he went to the room that was his special sanctum and closed the door behind him.

Zoia went to find Jacques.

"I think, Jacques, it is now time for us to leave Russia and for Papa to build up another orchestra somewhere else."

"I agree with you, *m'mselle*," Jacques replied. "What we have to decide is where to go and to persuade your father to leave."

"It will not be easy, but I will talk to him about it after dinner this evening."

"You do that, *m'mselle*, and I'll cook him a very special dinner, all the dishes he really enjoys!"

Jacques was a superb cook and Pierre Vallon, like every Frenchman, enjoyed his food.

That would set the scene, Zoia knew, and all she had to do was to try to persuade her father that his talents would be more appreciated somewhere else.

Then they would be off on their travels again.

Even as she thought about it, she found herself wishing that she could see the Duke just once more.

She wondered if he knew that she had left St. Petersburg. Perhaps he had come back to ask her to play to him again and learned that she had departed.

Without even closing her eyes, she could see his handsome face, his steel-grey eyes and the expression which was almost one of bewilderment as he asked her what had happened to him and why he had felt as he had.

'He understood Papa's music,' Zoia said beneath her breath, as if she reassured herself that it had been true.

The memory of the moment when their hands had touched and something magnetic and something inexplicable had passed between them that was unforgettable.

Slowly she walked up the stairs and because it was to be a very special dinner for her father and, because she had a feeling that it was an important one, she was deciding which of her gowns she would wear.

Her father always liked her to be well dressed as he had wanted her mother to be.

He had a Frenchman's appreciation for a woman who was elegant as well as beautiful, and, when she reached her bedroom, Zoia went to her wardrobe, opened it and looked at the gowns that hung there.

There were none of the gowns that she had worn in St. Petersburg because, as they had been creased through being packed, Maria had taken them to another room where she would press them before putting them into Zoia's wardrobe.

But there were several lovely gowns that she had left behind when she had gone to St. Petesburg and among them was one which she knew was her father's favourite.

'I will wear that one,' she told herself and could not help wondering whether, if the Duke could see her in it, he too would think it attractive.

Then she almost laughed at the idea that he would notice anything that she wore.

It had been obvious from the things the Princess had said that beautiful women fluttered around him not only in

St. Petersburg but especially in London where he was of great social standing.

Zoia felt her spirits drop.

'He will never think of me again,' she mused. 'Why should he?'

And, because it was so painful to think of her own insignificance, the sunshine seemed to have lost its brightness.

*

It was nearly four hours later and Zoia was now ready for dinner, which Jacques had said would be late because he had so much cooking to do.

She was putting the last touches to her hair when she heard a loud knocking on the front door.

It startled her and instantly the thought of the Grand Duke Boris sprang to her mind.

It was the way that his servants, as arrogant and imperious as their Master, had knocked day after day, often hour after hour, when she was in Moscow before.

'Surely he cannot have learnt that I am here already?' she asked herself.

Then she thought it extremely unlikely that the Grand Duke had remained in Moscow when all the other noble families had left.

The knocking came again and now Zoia rose from the stool in front of her dressing table and went to the top of the stairs.

Below she saw Jacques struggling into his uniform coat and pulling off the white apron that he had been cooking in and then hurrying across the hall to the front door.

He opened it and Zoia heard him speaking to someone outside in Russian.

She just could not hear what was being said, even though she leaned over the banisters, and then Jacques turned from the door and, looking up as if he had suspected that she would be there, he cried out,

"*M'mselle*, please come here at once!"

*

The Duke, travelling in a carriage drawn by six horses with a small troop of soldiers to escort him, drove towards Moscow at tremendous speed.

Like Prince Ysevolsov and all the other nobles, the Czar's horses were stabled along the road between St. Petersburg and Moscow and in His Imperial Majesty's case at much closer intervals than those of his subjects.

This meant that, with a frequent change of horses, the Duke was enabled to complete his journey in a far faster time than anyone else

He recalled that once Catharine the Great had reached Moscow in three days but for her the horses were changed every hour.

The Duke was a good traveller and constant swaying of the carriage, which many people found disagreeable, did not perturb him.

He slept some of the time and for the rest he had sat thinking a great deal about Zoia, in fact she continually impinged on his thoughts even when he wished to concentrate on the situation that he would find when he reached Borodino.

Actually, when he arrived, it was a few minutes after four o'clock and the overwhelming noise of guns which he had heard during the last hour of his journey had stopped.

He was, however, well aware that a tremendous battle had taken place for, as he drew nearer, he could see South of the road he had travelled on the fearful spectacle of a battlefield disappearing into a far horizon apparently covered with dead and wounded.

It was so horrifying that he found it difficult to believe that he was not seeing a vision rather than the actual truth of what had occurred.

When he alighted from his carriage, he saw a number of Staff Officers gathered on an incline above the road and below them were tens of thousands of men lying dead in various attitudes while wounded soldiers with scared faces were struggling to move away from their fallen comrades.

The Duke fortunately found General Kutuzov with the Officers and immediately made himself known to him.

Kutuzov was speaking quietly and without elation in his voice, but there was no doubt he was convinced that he had achieved a notable victory.

The Duke waited while the General finished dictating a despatch to the Czar and there was a young Officer waiting to carry it to St. Petersburg.

The Duke knew only too well that it would be received there with peals of bells from the Churches, fireworks, chains of lanterns along the banks of the River Neva and every vessel in the Port illuminated and beflagged.

He was certain that Kutuzov would be rewarded with a Princely title and a huge sum in roubles and doubtless a Marshal's baton as well.

He also thought, with inexpressible relief, that now Zoia would be safe in Moscow and, if he did not spend too long with the Russian Generals, there would be a chance of his seeing her tonight.

He distinctly liked the idea of being the person to inform her and her father that they and their home were safe.

He therefore congratulated General Kutuzov and his Staff and then went in search of Sir Robert Wilson.

He was not very far away and was obviously pleased to see the Duke.

"I was told you were in St. Petersburg, Your Grace," he said, "and I wondered how soon I should see you at the Front."

"It is quite obvious that I have arrived too late to be of any help," the Duke replied with a smile.

Sir Robert, however, looked grave.

"I would hope that General Kutuzov is not sending despatches to the Czar claiming an overwhelming victory?"

"That is exactly what he has done," the Duke replied.

He saw the frown between Sir Robert's eyes and asked him abruptly,

"Are you telling me that such an assumption is premature?"

"I believe so."

"Why?"

"Because the cost of the battle is inconceivable."

The Duke looked grave.

'What have you lost?" he asked.

"It is absolutely impossible to calculate the number of men killed at present," Sir Robert replied, "but at a very conservative estimate the Russian Army must have lost forty thousand men."

"Impossible!" the Duke gasped.

"I may be wrong, I hope to God I am!" Sir Robert said, "But you only have to look at the battlefield to see the devastation in front of you and the guns have all been firing since six o'clock this morning."

"That would be for ten hours," the Duke calculated.

"Exactly," Sir Robert agreed.

"And what are the French losses?"

"That we don't know. They will be heavy too, very heavy."

It was obvious that Sir Robert had no more to tell him and the Duke went back to the road where his carriage was waiting amongst a *mêlée* of soldiers being re-grouped, wounded being lifted onto stretchers and horses being employed to move the guns.

The Duke was just about to step into his carriage and to tell the coachman to drive on to Moscow when he saw another vehicle approaching on the road and he recognised the livery of the coachmen on the box.

As the four horses drew nearer, he could see that he was not mistaken and it was Prince Vsevolsov's carriage, which he was sure was the one that had carried Zoia to Moscow.

He walked down the road towards it and, putting up his hand, caused the coachman to draw the horses to a standstill.

The footman on the box recognised the Duke and jumped down and another man riding with the escort did the same thing.

The servants greeted him respectfully and the Duke asked,

"You have taken Miss Zoia Vallon to her father's house in Moscow I believe?"

"That is right, Your Excellency."

"Will you give me the address?" the Duke enquired.

The man was about to reply when two horses pulling a gun forced them to move aside to let it pass.

There were several Russian soldiers in charge of it, all giving orders at the same time and the Duke could see that they were covered in dust and dirt and looked very tired to the point of exhaustion.

The wheels stuck in the ground and before the horses could proceed an Officer came up to demand,

"What are you doing? Where are you going with that gun?"

"We were told to move it, sir," one of the soldiers answered, "because there be a shell stuck in the barrel and it can't be fired."

"What do you mean it cannot be fired?" the Officer questioned aggressively.

"It's stuck, sir."

"Then fire it! We cannot have the guns moved from their positions in case the French attack us again."

Looking at the sea of dead bodies between the Russians' present position and the French on the horizon the Duke thought that this was unlikely, but the Officer, fussily authoritative, insisted,

"Fire the gun *now*! Fire it in the direction of the enemy. If it kills a few more of those damned invaders, all the better!"

One of the men obediently forced a ramrod down the barrel of the gun saying as he did so,

"We've tried this a dozen times, sir. The shell won't budge."

"Then try it again!" the Officer snapped.

They obeyed him.

Then there was a huge explosion and, to the Duke watching, the whole world seemed to burst into flames —

*

Zoia reached the front door and saw, standing outside on the steps, two of the servants who had brought her to Moscow.

She was somewhat surprised to see them, thinking that by now they would already be on their journey home.

However she smiled at them, saying,

"Good evening. Is anything wrong?"

"It's just that we didn't know what else to do with His Excellency, *m'mselle*," the elder of the two men responded in broken French.

Zoia did not understand and Jacques explained,

"They say, *m'mselle*, that the gentleman was tellin' them that he was comin' to see you when a cannon accidentally exploded. Three soldiers were then killed, one of His Highness's servants and his horse and the gentleman's valet. The gentleman himself is badly wounded."

Zoia felt as if her heart was constricted and it was hard to breathe.

"What – gentleman?" she asked, but she already knew the answer.

She ran down the steps as fast as she could and across the pavement.

She could see that the side of the carriage had been badly damaged by fragments from the explosion and, as the door was opened, she looked inside to see the Duke lying on the back seat covered in blood.

"His Highness's house here in Moscow is now closed and everyone has left," one of the servants said beside her in an apologetic tone. "We didn't know where else to take him."

"You were right to – bring him here," Zoia told him.

Turning to Jacques she asked him,

"Tell them to move him carefully – very carefully."

It was not until the men had carried the Duke upstairs and laid him on the bed in the only unoccupied bedroom in the small house that Zoia, looking frantically at Maria, asked,

"He is – not dead?"

It was not surprising that she should put the question for the Duke's face was devoid of all colour, his eyes were closed, his whole body was limp and it appeared as if he had no life left in him.

"He's not dead yet, *m'mselle*, and if it be God's will, we'll keep him alive," Maria said briskly.

She immediately took charge in the practical manner of a Frenchwoman confronted with a situation which could not be hopeless as long as there was something that could be done.

The Prince's servants were told to find a doctor. Jacques gave them several addresses in case the doctors, as well as everybody else, had left Moscow.

Zoia was sent to the kitchen to boil water while Maria and Jacques undressed the Duke to ascertain the extent of his wounds.

When Zoia came upstairs with the kettle, a basin and a number of linen towels, the Duke was between the sheets and, she felt, looking even paler and more lifeless than he had before.

Now her father was here and his calm acceptance of the situation was more comforting than anything he might say,

"A doctor should be here soon," he said as if Zoia had asked him the question. "They will not all have left Moscow. In fact I know that the wounded are being taken to the empty houses of those who have run away."

Even as he spoke there was a knock on the door.

*

It was after eleven o'clock when Zoia and her father sat down in the dining room to a somewhat inadequate meal. They had not thought of eating while there was so much to do for the Duke.

"You met His Grace in St. Petersburg?" Pierre Vallon asked her,

"Yes, he came to visit the Princess when Tania and I were – dancing in the little theatre."

Pierre Vallon looked at his daughter and they were too close for him not to realise that the way she spoke merely confirmed the impression that he had gained when he had seen her looking at the Duke upstairs.

"You mean something to each other?" he asked her quietly.

"It was – very strange. Papa, but the moment I – met him I knew that he was – different from any man I had ever met before."

"In what way?"

"For one thing, he understood your music and, when I played to him – he saw what we had – seen."

There was no need to say anything more. Pierre Vallon understood so much that was not expressed in words.

"You are sure?" he asked.

"Quite, quite sure, Papa. You know I would not be mistaken – about anything like that. Besides the next day when he called and found me alone, he asked me what I had – done to him. He said that he had never felt like – that in his – whole life."

"It's extraordinary," Pierre Vallon murmured,

"That he should feel like – that?"

"That the Duke of Welminster should," her father replied, "I met His Grace while I was in London and again in Vienna. From all I have heard about him, and people talk about him quite a lot, I should not have imagined for one moment that he would be as you say he is."

Zoia smiled.

"You well know I could never be mistaken, Papa, and no one – no one but you has ever – understood before."

Pierre Vallon did not answer for a moment and then he said,

"You know, my dearest, that I would never doubt anything you might tell me or interfere unnecessarily with any friendship you might make, but, if your mother was alive, I feel sure that she would explain to you that the Duke of Welminster can mean nothing in your life."

"I have – thought of that, Papa."

"It would be best," Pierre Vallon said slowly, "if tomorrow I arrange for His Grace to be moved into a hospital. There must be one where he can have every attention, perhaps better than we can give him here."

Zoia was silent for a moment.

Then she said,

"In a way, Papa, I feel – responsible for what has happened. His Highness's servants said that the Duke was asking for my address – when the gun exploded."

Her father did not reply, but she was well aware that he was thinking that the Duke had no right to intrude on their private life and no right to pursue a girl who did not belong to his own Social world.

Zoia gave up pretending to eat and clasped her hands together.

"When you fell in love with Mama," she asked him in a low voice, "did you have any – choice as to whether you – loved her or whether you did – not?"

Pierre Vallon looked at his daughter and there was no mistaking the consternation in his expression.

"Are you telling me that you love this man? "

"*Yes* – Papa"

"But how can you be sure? You have seen him twice, perhaps three times."

Zoia smiled and it seemed to illuminate her face.

"Really, Papa!" she scolded him. "How can you, of all people, ask that – question and expect me to answer it?"

"In my case it was different," Pierre Vallon said.

"Was it?" Zoia queried. "Mama said that from the moment she saw you she fell in love with you and – she thought that you loved her too at that instant."

"How could I help it?" he asked. "She was so lovely and so exquisite in every way. And, my dearest, you are very like her."

"Not only in my features and my eyes, although I have your fair hair – but in the – things I feel."

She gave a little laugh that seemed to ring out so spontaneously that her father found himself smiling too.

"How can you expect me to be anything – but your daughter?" she asked. "I see what you see when you play, hear what you hear and try to express myself as you do in music. But I am also – Mama's child."

Her voice softened as she went on,

"As you know, Papa, my heart has never been touched – until this moment. That is why the Grand Duke and a number of other people call me the *Ice Maiden*. But from the moment I – looked into the Duke of Welminster's eyes from – the moment I touched his hand, the ice – melted and – I was in love!"

"Do you understand, my dearest, that there can be no happy ending to the story?" Pierre Vallon asked.

His voice was filled with pain as if he hated to know how much she would suffer.

"I am aware of that," Zoia replied. "But it still does not prevent me – from loving him, even though I am sure that he will never love me – in the same way."

"I will arrange for him to go to the hospital."

"*No*, Papa."

"In this you must be guided by me. I don't wish to hurt you. You know I want only your happiness, but for him to stay here is madness and I cannot contemplate where that madness would end."

Zoia knew that he was saying without words and telling her that what the Duke would offer her would not be marriage.

She gave a deep sigh.

"I know that you are – thinking of me, Papa," she said quietly, "but every instinct in my body tells me to look after the Duke and nurse him – back to health."

"And every instinct in mine is to protect you," Pierre Vallon retorted, "to keep you from making yourself eventually much more unhappy than you will be if you say 'goodbye' to him now. Just think of what has happened as a dream, a fantasy that has brought you something beautiful, just as music will bring you the same inspiration."

He paused for a moment before he went on,

"If you don't see the Duke, if we leave him here in Moscow as I intend, then gradually the feelings he has evoked in you and the image of him you have in your mind will vanish."

He made a gesture with his hands as he added,

"Of course the music you have played for him will bring it back and you will always have a certain nostalgia for the moment in your life when you first fell in love, but there will be other loves and other moments that I promise you!"

"How can you be sure?" Zoia asked him. "If, when you left Prince Strovolsky's Palace, Mama had not gone with you, would you have forgotten her?"

She knew as she saw her father's face that he wanted to lie, but he was unable to do so.

"Was your love for Mama really different from – what I feel for the Duke?" Zoia asked, pressing home her point.

Her father did not answer and she went on,

"You have taught me, Papa, to analyse – my own feelings. You have also taught me to distinguish what is real and what is true from what is false and I know what – I feel now is not the adolescent romancing I sometimes indulged in years ago. This is as real as breathing, hearing – and seeing."

She gave a little sigh as she went on,

"If the Duke never spoke to me again and if, as you suggest, I never – saw him again, I should still love him and I am absolutely certain in my own mind that I shall never feel this way for – anyone else."

There was a silence that seemed full of a thousand unspoken words.

Then Pierre Vallon admitted,

"I don't know what to say to you, my dearest."

"Then shall we leave things alone for the moment and – nurse the Duke back to health? Then we will face the fact that I must go out of his life – and I expect eventually he will want to go out of mine."

"I would still like to look for a hospital," Pierre Vallon said. "I promise I will do nothing without consulting you first, but I have a feeling that the Duke may be ill for longer than I wish to stay in Moscow."

"You intend to leave – so quickly?"

"I want to go," Pierre Vallon replied. "After the slaughter there must have been today on the battlefield, I shall feel uncomfortably self-conscious of being French."

It was not only that, Zoia thought to herself, because his nationality had never worried him before. It was because he was bitterly disappointed and hurt that his orchestra had left without telling him and deserted it seemed in the very moment of victory.

She could understand how in their hour of fear they had wanted to take their wives and children out of the City, which might be invaded by the French.

They would now return, she told herself, and, if they apologised to her father he would forgive them for he was the type of man who could never bear a grudge for long.

At the same time she knew how deeply he would feel if he had been abandoned by those he had trusted and she thought perhaps that even they had said to themselves,

'After all he is only a Frenchman. Why should we trouble about him?'

Dinner was now finished and Zoia, without making any excuse, went up the stairs to see the Duke.

Maria was with him and, when Zoia appeared in the doorway, she came out of the room into the passage.

"How is – he?" Zoia asked.

"It's difficult to tell, *m'mselle*. The doctor is comin' again tomorrow and hopes to bring with him someone who is more experienced in such bad injuries than he is. That is if there is anyone left in Moscow."

"Did the doctor – say that?"

"He said that people have been leavin' here every day and every hour and apart from anythin' else, it's impossible to find supplies for the wounded."

"I cannot understand how they can be such cowards," Zoia asserted indignantly.

Maria put out her hand consolingly.

"Don't you worry, *m'mselle*. We'll look after the gentleman one way or another. He's a strong man and that will count in his favour more than anythin' else."

Zoia's eyes searched the older woman's face.

"Are you telling me that his life is really in danger?"

For a moment Maria hesitated and then she told her the truth,

"He's bad, *m'mselle*, but not so bad we cannot save him with careful nursin'."

She saw Zoia's face and added quickly,

"Now don't you go upsettin' yourself. He'll run a high fever, there's no doubt about that. And there's nothin' you can do about it. But Jacques and I will look after him. You can trust us."

"You must let me help too," Zoia suggested swiftly. "I may not be as experienced – as you, Maria, but I know I can help him. I really know that I can give him some of my – own strength."

She did not wait for Maria's reply, but passing her she went into the bedroom.

The Duke was lying very still and again Zoia thought, with a constriction of her heart, that he might be dead.

Then she reached out her hand and touched his and felt that there was still some warmth in it.

It was like seeing a great oak tree fallen to the ground to see him so quiet and so lifeless.

Then with both her hands holding his, she felt as if she poured the life force from her own body into him.

She could feel her spirit reaching out to his spirit and at the same time she knew that her heart was searching for his heart and offering him her love unconditionally.

'Oh, God, make him well and strong – again', she prayed. 'He must live. Don't take life from him – but let him live.'

It was a prayer that came from the very depths of her being, a prayer that strained every nerve and every feeling within her.

Then she said aloud to the Duke,

"I love you – think of me – come to me – I am yours – and I so want you – to live."

There was, of course, no response from the Duke.

But she felt in some way that she could not interpret in whatever darkness and oblivion he lay she had enveloped him in her love and she could somehow reach him.

CHAPTER SIX

"The smell of burning is worse!"

The Duke spoke in a low voice and at the first sound Zoia rose from the armchair where she had been sitting and went to his bedside to say,

"I thought you were – asleep."

He looked up at her, thinking that her hair silhouetted against the sunlight coming from the windows formed a golden halo around her head.

Then he persisted,

"You are not answering my question. The smell is worse than it has been at any time."

"I think the wooden houses in the – next street are on fire," Zoia replied.

"I have already said that you and your father must leave Moscow at once," the Duke said. "I am sure that the doctor can find somewhere for me to go and I must not keep you here any longer."

He spoke with an effort, but his tone was firm.

Zoia smiled.

"Do you think we could – desert you or hand you over as a – prisoner to the French?"

"It has to be done. When the doctor comes again, I will order him to find somewhere for me to go."

Zoia did not reply for a moment.

She was thinking of the twenty-five thousand wounded Russian soldiers who had been brought into Moscow after the battle.

The Government had reacted by claiming that there was no proper accommodation for them in the City, nor could they be attended to and they were to be sent away to other towns.

Once the order had been given, it was found that there were no vehicles to evacuate them in and, although some had got away, ten thousand Russians remained in Moscow before the French brought in their own wounded.

Even now it was difficult for Zoia or anyone else to believe that Moscow, the Holy City of Russia, had been evacuated without a shot being fired in its defence.

The French had arrived to find the place practically deserted and Pierre Vallon had been told that Napoleon was stunned by the emptiness of the streets and by the abandoned houses and shops.

Only the very poorest and aged who had no means of transport had remained and they had crowded into the many Churches for safety.

After the French had moved in, the soldiers, completely out of control, began looting and soon, because there was plenty of wine available, became hopelessly drunk.

Fire had broken out amongst the wooden houses, but no one seemed to know if it had been a deliberate action on the part of the Russians or whether it was accidental.

Zoia had learned from Jacques that large parts of the City were already in ruins and the conflagration was worse because, when the Russians had left, they had taken the fire engines and the hoses with them.

At night when everything was quiet, standing at her open window, Zoia could hear in the distance the rumbling of falling walls and the excited shouts of the French soldiers.

In the daytime there was no escaping from the smell of the smoke or the sight of it, thick and black, rising above the roofs.

She knew that her father was afraid of what would happen to them and the reports that Jacques had brought back from the centre of the City, where the French were encamped, were more and more depressing and discouraging.

"I must get you away," Pierre Vallon said not once but a hundred times to his daughter.

"So how could we leave the Duke, Papa, even if it was possible for us to escape?" Zoia would ask.

Last night, when they had the same conversation, Pierre Vallon had risen from the table where they had been sitting to say sharply,

"Pack everything that is of vital necessity."

Zoia had looked at him apprehensively.

"What do you intend to do, Papa?"

"I intend to take you away before the house is burnt down over our heads or worse still the soldiers break down the door in search of loot."

Zoia heard the fear in his voice and knew that he was afraid not for himself but for her.

Quietly she answered,

"I will go with you, Papa, but we *must* take the Duke with us."

Her father did not reply.

This morning when he left the house he had kissed her and urged her,

"Keep the door securely locked and you and Maria be ready to leave at the first possible opportunity. I am taking Jacques with me to make the necessary arrangements."

"With whom, Papa?" Zoia asked, but he had not answered her.

She locked the door behind him. It was now the back door they used for Jacques had boarded up the front door of the house so that it looked as if it was unoccupied.

The looting soldiers were usually in such a total drunken state that they did not trouble, Jacques said, to force their way into any building that was difficult, preferring houses like those of the nobles, which had simply been abandoned with full cellars.

It seemed incredible after all General Kutuzov had said about 'defending Moscow to the last drop of my blood' that he should have withdrawn his Army and left the road clear for Napoleon and the French to march into the ancient City.

But the enormous casualties the Russians had suffered had made it impossible for him to attack the French or even defend the City.

When the Duke had recovered consciousness and was well enough to understand what had occurred, he had realised that Sir Robert Wilson had been nearly right in what he had anticipated that the casualties would be.

Forty-three thousand Russians had been killed or wounded and thirty thousand French.

The report of a great victory, which General Kutuzov had despatched so quickly to the Czar, was a hollow triumph when Moscow had to be abandoned.

Pierre Vallon, perhaps because he was French, realised what a desperate disappointment his entry into the hallowed Capital had been to Napoleon.

There had been for him almost a mystic significance in the thought of finding the five hundred domes gilded or painted in brilliant colours waiting for him, only to discover a week later that he was only in possession of a heap of smouldering ruins.

"What will the Emperor do now, Papa?" Zoia had asked.

"I am sure he expects that the Czar will ask for an Armistice."

Zoia had repeated this conversation to the Duke and he had said after thinking over what she had told him,

"I believe that the loss of Moscow will have a traumatic effect on the Czar and on the Russian people."

"What do you mean – by that?" Zoia had enquired.

"I have a feeling that the yawning gap between the nobles and the peasants will be closed at least for a time and the Czar, fortified by the deep religious fervour which possesses him at the moment, will refuse to negotiate."

"What makes you so sure it will happen?" Zoia asked.

He looked at her with his grey eyes and replied quietly,

"Ever since I have known you, I have felt as if I had a 'sixth sense' that I have never used before."

She gave a little sigh.

"I knew you had that when you – listened to me playing and you – understood what Papa had meant when he wrote the music."

"I don't understand it myself," the Duke muttered reflectively.

Then he closed his eyes as if he was too weak to go on with the conversation.

*

For the first three days after coming to Pierre Vallon's house, he had been desperately ill and had run, as Maria had anticipated, a very high fever.

She and Jacques had sponged him down regularly with vinegar and, although she had not admitted it to Zoia, Maria thought at times that there was nothing they could do to save his life.

But he had survived and the doctor ascribed it to his being so fit.

"A very strong young man," he had observed with some satisfaction.

Zoia, however, believed that it was the Life Force that she had poured into him whenever they were alone.

"You must get well," she had said to him in her soft voice as he lay unconscious. "You are wanted in the world. There is so much for you to do. Come back! Come back from wherever you are!"

She felt as if she called on his spirit with her own and, as every day he grew stronger, she was sure that she sustained and strengthened him in a manner that would be laughed at by medical science.

Now he was better, but still very weak and she wondered, although she did not say so aloud, whether a long journey would be too much for him even provided that her father could take him away.

She knew how fanatically Napoleon loathed the English, who had frustrated him at every turn and it would be inconceivable to leave the Duke a prisoner in French hands.

He was apparently asleep when she heard the knock on the back door which told her that her father and Jacques had returned.

Quietly she left the bedroom and then sped down the stairs to find, when she reached the kitchen, that Maria had already let in the two men.

Because every time Pierre Vallon left the house there was always the fear that he might not return, Zoia ran towards him to put her arms around his neck and kiss his cheek as he told her,

"I have good news!"

"What is it, Papa?"

"I have obtained from the Emperor himself not only a permit to leave the City but the promise that we shall have an escort until we are outside the walls."

Zoia did not speak. She only waited and Pierre Vallon added with a faint smile,

"The permit includes you and me, Maria and Jacques and a member of my orchestra who was unfortunately hurt by the collapse of a burning house."

Zoia gave a little cry of sheer relief.

"Oh, Papa! How did you manage it and how dared you go to see the Emperor himself?"

"I asked to see him and he remembered me. We talked of the last time I played in Paris and then I explained to him the predicament I was in because you were with me."

Zoia made a little sound, but she did not interrupt and Pierre Vallon went on,

"The Emperor said, 'I can understand your anxiety and I suppose that I must let you go, although I would have liked you to stay and play for me. 'I hope to do that in happier times, Your Majesty,' I answered. 'I look forward to it,' the Emperor said. 'The Opera House in Paris is waiting for you'."

Zoia clasped her hands together.

"That was very complimentary, Papa, but how will we be able to get away?"

"Jacques has kept our two carriages well hidden, which was fortunate because practically every vehicle in the City was commandeered by those who left before the French arrived."

"And horses?" Zoia asked.

"They too are in a safe place," her father answered. "I have decided that it would be best for us to leave at dawn. The Emperor has promised us an escort of soldiers and we are less likely at such an early hour to become involved with those who are robbing anyone they find on the streets."

He thought as he spoke of the horrifying spectacles that he had witnessed when he and Jacques had gone to the Kremlin to find the Emperor.

Everywhere they looked they had seen French soldiers staggering from houses laden not only with money and jewels but with boots, linen, women's furs and cloaks.

They had seen people in the streets robbed of their clothes with those resisting being savagely beaten.

They had learned that the French were pillaging the Churches and any woman who was not old and decrepit was seized and carried away regardless of her shrieks and struggles.

Although Pierre Vallon did not say so, the flames of the burning City were now coming perilously close to the quiet little square where he had bought his wife her 'doll's house'.

Zoia went upstairs and, when she then entered the Duke's bedroom, she saw that he was awake and was watching her as she moved towards him.

"You have news?" he asked.

She did not ask him how he knew for she was aware that they were so closely attuned that he knew what she was thinking as he had been when she played the piano.

"We leave at dawn tomorrow morning."

"*We?*"

"Papa has a special permit from the Emperor Bonaparte himself for us to leave the City and we are to be escorted by soldiers."

"He has seen the Emperor?"

The Duke did not seem surprised.

"Yes and he remembered him."

There was a faint smile on the Duke's lips as he replied,

"Who could forget Pierre Vallon?"

As he spoke, Zoia wondered if, when he was well, he would forget her, but she dared not ask the question.

"Where are we going?" the Duke enquired now.

Zoia looked startled.

"I forgot to ask Papa. It did not seem important – as long as we leave Moscow."

"Tell your father to make for Odessa. I know the Governor and it should be easy from there to find a ship to carry us home."

The Duke closed his eyes again as if talking was still an effort and Zoia stood indecisive beside the bed.

'To carry us home!'

'Did he mean by that to *his* home? To England?' she asked herself.

She longed to ask him to explain and then she was afraid of the likely answer.

Of course what he really meant was, because England had command of the seas, there would be English ships that would be only too honoured to carry back to their own country anyone as important as the Duke.

But to the English she and her father were the enemies. Because she felt that there was nothing she could say, Zoia went to her own room, which was just across the passage, and started to add to the things she had already packed.

Suddenly she felt that the only way that she could express the conflict which raged within her was in music.

Because she felt, when the Duke was unconscious, that music might reach him when the human voice could not do so, she had persuaded Jacques to bring the piano that was usually housed in the salon up to her bedroom.

There were two pianos in the house. The one that her father preferred was in his special sanctum. The other one, that she and her mother would play, was also used to entertain their friends, who would seldom leave the house without begging Pierre Vallon to let them hear one of his compositions.

It stood now in an alcove in her bedroom and, knowing that the doors of both rooms were open so that the Duke could listen, Zoia sat down on the stool.

She started to play very softly the music that she had been playing that very first day in the Ysevolsov Palace when he had come to listen to her and had known what she was seeing as she played.

The melody composed by her father swept away her fears for the future and made her forget for a moment the fires raging outside and the smoke billowing up into the sky.

She was again transported into a magical world of beauty and happiness and only as she finished playing did she wonder if the Duke was asleep or whether he was listening as he had done before and understood.

As she wondered, she heard him call her name.

She ran from the piano across the passage and into his room.

She went to his bedside, he put out his hand and she laid hers in it.

"You were playing for me?" he asked in a deep voice.

"Yes."

"I thought so and I remember just how shocked I was the first time that it should have aroused such unusual feelings in me."

"And – now?"

"I think it was Fate that brought us together and Fate that we should not only meet but be here when history is being made, something that we shall both of us remember for the rest of our lives."

Because his fingers were holding hers, it was difficult for Zoia to think of anything but the magic that she felt within herself because they were touching each other.

She was sure that the Duke was too ill to feel, as had happened before when their hands touched, a magnetic rapture that was indescribable.

But she realised that his eyes were on her face and she thought that they were searching for something, but she was not certain what it was.

"Once we are free of Moscow, we will move very slowly," she said, "so that you will not be bumped unnecessarily or suffer too much discomfort."

"I know that you and Maria will look after me and I am so relieved that, owing to your father's cleverness, you are able to escape from Moscow."

Zoia looked down at him a little uncertainly.

She thought because his words were so formal that she could not understand what he was thinking.

She had an impulse to go down on her knees beside the bed and tell him how much she loved him and that she would sacrifice her life willingly if it would make him better or keep him safe.

Then she thought perhaps he would be embarrassed and would suggest that she behave in a more restrained manner.

She released her hand and, walking to the window, stood looking out blindly.

Then she saw that behind the houses on the other side of the square that there was the brilliant light of a raging fire and she could even see flames rising every now and then above the grey of the buildings.

She heard her father coming up the stairs and a moment later he walked into the room.

"Zoia will have told Your Grace the news," he addressed the Duke.

"As I said to you before," he replied, "you will travel more safely and perhaps a great deal faster without me."

"On the contrary," Pierre Vallon replied, "I intend to go to Odessa and we will then need your assistance to find some way of reaching France."

Zoia started.

So that was where he wished to go, back to their home in France.

"I am sure that something can be arranged," the Duke answered.

Zoia knew by the way he spoke that he was desperately tired.

"I think it would be wise," she suggested, "if I asked Jacques to cook you something light and then you went to sleep as soon as possible. We all have to rise very early tomorrow morning.

The Duke did not reply and without troubling him further Zoia went downstairs in search of Jacques.

*

When they were clear of Moscow and the four horses pulling their carriage were moving at a good rate, Zoia gave a sign of relief that seemed to come from the very depths of her being.

Outside the windows there was the unspoilt Russian countryside and there were only a few people on the road.

She wondered why they were going to Odessa until her father explained to her why he had made the decision.

"It would be impossible to travel into Europe accompanied by an Englishman," he said, "and I also think we are wise to travel South where the weather will be warmer than it is likely to be here in a very short time."

"That is true," Zoia agreed. "It often becomes very cold in October."

"Last year it snowed at the end of September," her father replied, "and that is something the Emperor would be wise to remember."

Zoia had been surprised when morning came to find that her father, or perhaps Jacques, had engaged no less than eight servants to accompany them.

She did not ask where these Russians had been hiding, but thought perhaps that it was in the same place where Jacques had concealed their carriages and horses, which were strong and well-bred.

Because she was so close to her father, she knew that he was feeling apprehensive that the soldiers in their escort might take it upon themselves to commandeer the horses, which, after the slaughter at Borodino, were obviously in short supply.

But the French soldiers were not inclined or reckless enough to do anything but obey the orders they had been given and soon after dawn they started to move towards the Rogozhskol Gate which would take them out of the West side of the City.

Fortunately this did not require them to pass through the centre where most of the troops were quartered.

Nevertheless it was a most nerve-racking drive as, apart from the fear that some officious Frenchman might challenge them, or a mob of drunken soldiers decide to pilfer the carriages, there was also the danger of the burning houses and the falling walls.

As they drove along, it looked to Zoia as if at least three-quarters of the houses they passed were in flames, but Jacques had said that there were still parts of Moscow that had not been damaged.

But at times she could feel the burning heat of the flames almost scorching her face and, when they reached the bridge over the river, her father looked back with an expression that made her ask quickly,

"What has upset you, Papa?"

"The Grand Theatre was burning last night"

"Oh, Papa, I am sorry."

"It is not surprising. It was built of wood and a year's supply of timber had been stacked against the walls."

He spoke almost without expression in his voice, but she knew how much it hurt him.

Again he was thinking of her mother and how pleased she had been when they first came to Moscow because the theatre had seemed to be an ideal place for him to build up a great orchestra in exactly the way he wanted it.

Deliberately, because she wanted to cheer him up, Zoia made her voice sound light and almost happy as she tried to reassure him,

"We are starting a new chapter of our lives, Papa, and I have a feeling that it will be an exhilarating and exciting one for you."

Her father did not reply and she could not help remembering that she could not say the same thing for herself. But she knew that what mattered for the moment, more than anything else, was that the Duke was safe and that he still needed her.

Jacques had constructed a very comfortable bed in the larger of Pierre Vallon's carriages, using a board of wood stretching from the back seat onto the smaller one opposite.

He had heaped on it two comfortable mattresses and, with the help of their new servants, they had carried the Duke downstairs.

Careful though they had been, Zoia knew that the Duke found it extremely painful.

She had seen his lips tighten and the colour leave his face, but he said nothing except to thank those who had carried him to the carriage.

There was room for her to sit beside him and her father to sit on the small seat opposite, but she was determined that, once they were out of the City, she would persuade her father to drive in the other carriage.

This, at the moment, contained only Maria and a number of small packages and parcels that she had insisted on taking with them at the last moment.

Their trunks had been strapped on the top of the two carriages and Zoia could not help thinking it was fortunate that the Russians could not see the very elegant clothing that the Duke owned.

After his valet had been killed by the explosion, Prince Ysevolsov's servants had been sensible enough to take all the Duke's possessions from the Czar's carriage.

The chief servant who had escorted her to Moscow had been in the Prince's employment for many years and he understood the needs of a gentleman.

It would have been difficult otherwise, Zoia thought, to provide the Duke, who was so tall and broad-shouldered, with the clothes that he would need once he was on his feet again.

She and Maria had packed only the essentials for themselves for the journey.

There were many little things that Zoia would have liked to take with her because they reminded her of her mother or simply because she was so fond of them, but she knew that to overload the horses on such a long journey might easily prevent them from reaching their destination safely.

She therefore restricted herself to packing only what she thought she would actually need and just a few of her prettiest gowns that were light and took up very little room.

What was more important than anything else was that they should have enough food for Jacques thought that it might be difficult to buy much on the journey.

"People are frightened when there's a war that they themselves will go hungry," he said to Zoia. "I can't have the Master gettin' ill, or you, *m'mselle*, for that matter."

He did not include the Duke in his solicitude and Zoia knew without being told that Jacques almost resented the strange man who, he felt, had intruded on the family atmosphere that had been so evident in their small household before the Duke had joined it.

"You must not forget our invalid, Jacques," she said aloud.

"We'll not do that, *m'mselle*," Jacques nodded.

But his voice was cold and had none of the warmth in it that she would have liked to hear.

Maria, however, thought that the Duke was the finest man she had ever seen and, when he thanked her in his quiet voice for dressing his wounds and knowing that he was suffering acutely, she was overwhelmed by his bravery.

She would, Zoia knew, have done anything in her power to help him. But it was Jacques who was really responsible for the whole organisation of their journey from the moment they left Moscow.

When they were finally out of sight of the City and its spires and domes were no longer visible and there was only a great crimson glow in the sky from the fires, Pierre Vallon had an expression on his face that told Zoia that a composition was forming in his mind.

She knew the signs so well and, as soon as it was possible, she stopped the carriage and persuaded her father to change places with Maria.

If he was composing, he would want to be alone and she felt too that not only would he be more comfortable but she would be able to talk to the Duke without the feeling that every word they said to each other was overheard.

From the moment Pierre Vallon had realised that it would be impossible for the Duke to leave them without the certainty of being arrested and maybe killed for being English, he had not referred to Zoia's feelings for him again.

She knew, however, that he was still afraid that she would break her heart over a man who could never really be of any consequence in her life.

But, as if he realised that further discussion would only disrupt the closeness of their own relationship and anyway have little effect, Pierre Vallon had, in his characteristic manner, tried to divorce his mind from the problem.

It would be a great relief, Zoia told herself, if he could really concentrate on his music, because that meant that she would no longer feel guilty or that she was in any way defying her father whom she loved so devotedly.

The carriages started off again and Maria, after fussing a little over the Duke, sat back and almost immediately fell asleep.

Travelling by carriage always made her sleepy and Zoia thought with a little smile that now she was to all intents and purposes alone with the man she loved.

She expected him to sleep, but, when she looked again at the Duke, she found that he was watching her with his grey eyes.

"You are comfortable?" she asked.

"I am thinking how fortunate I am not to have been left to die at Borodino."

"Forget about it," Zoia said. "I have told Papa that — we are starting a new chapter in our lives and so I don't want to think anymore of the terrible casualties to both Armies or that Moscow is burning."

The Duke did not answer and after a moment she commented,

"There will be problems in the future, of course, but they will be new problems and perhaps we shall feel like the snakes who shed their old skins and emerge with new ones."

"I like your skin just as it is," the Duke murmured quietly.

She blushed because she was not expecting a compliment from him.

After a moment he went on,

"You are very remarkable, Zoia. I know of no other woman who would take what has happened these past few weeks so calmly or leave her home to burn to the ground without complaining about it with tears."

"I mind – of course I mind," Zoia replied, "but I have saved the only things that are of any importance to me – Papa – and *you*!"

She said the last two words very softly and did not look at the Duke as she spoke, but she was aware that his eyes were on her face and she wondered what he was thinking.

After a silence of some minutes, she turned to look at him and saw that once again he was asleep.

*

Afterwards it was difficult for Zoia to remember the details of the long journey between Moscow and Odessa.

They could not travel very far every day because the horses had to rest and there was no possibility of changing them as there had been on the journey from St. Petersburg,

In fact, owing to the War, horses were in such short supply that one of the servants had to be on watch every night for fear that the horses might be stolen or worse still they might be attacked by robbers.

When they went further South, it grew much warmer and there were vineyards where the grapes were being harvested in the hot sunshine. There was plentiful fruit on the trees and flowers everywhere so that Zoia found it enchanting.

Soon there were no further obvious signs of war, of soldiers being marched to the North to join Kutuzov's Army or only women working in the fields as their men had been taken from them for Military service.

Instead there were peasants who greeted them with smiles and were willing to sell them any fresh food they wished to buy.

The horses were now growing tired, but Zoia felt a new vitality and new energy seeping through her.

She knew it sprang from her happiness that the Duke was with her and every day he seemed to grow stronger.

They would talk together or sit in silence and yet know that they were communicating without words and there was a closeness between them that she dare not try to analyse.

Jacques had brought two tents where they could sleep at night or, if it seemed easier and more comfortable, she and Maria shared one carriage while her father slept beside the Duke.

It was then that Zoia would lie awake in the darkness and know that her love for the Duke had increased every hour and every minute that she had been beside him.

It was not what he said and it was not for any reason that she could explain rationally to herself.

It was just because her whole being went out towards him as the man she had always wanted to find and the man she had loved secretly in her music long before she met him.

'I am happy,' she thought, 'happier than I have ever been in my whole life and, as far as I am concerned, this journey can go on for ever into Eternity and I shall be content!'

But finally, because everything must come to an end, they saw Odessa ahead of them and her father announced when they were lunching beside the road,

"We will take Your Grace to the Governor General's Palace and then Zoia and I will find somewhere to stay."

Zoia started at her father's words and, without realising that she was doing so, looked pleadingly at the Duke.

"What are you saying?" the Duke enquired. "Of course you must come with me. As you must be aware, I cannot possibly do without you."

"I think it would be better, Your Grace, if we stayed on our own," Pierre Vallon replied. "After all for all you know the Governor-General may look on me as an enemy of his people, which indeed my countrymen are."

The Duke smiled.

"The Governor-General is, in fact, a Frenchman."

Pierre Vallon looked astonished and the Duke then explained,

"The Duc de Richelieu was an *émigré* during the French Revolution and entered Russian service. He became Governor General of New Russia, as they call the Ukraine, in 1803 and has been responsible for the development of the Port of Odessa, which I know will impress you."

As Pierre Vallon still looked surprised, the Duke finished by saying,

"I am assured that you will both find a warm welcome waiting for you at The Palace."

But Pierre Vallon still hesitated before he retreated,

"If you will promise me that we are not of the slightest embarrassment to Your Grace, then Zoia and I will be honoured to accompany you."

"May I also tell you," the Duke said, "that the Governor-General is extremely musical. In fact last time I was in Odessa some years ago, I remember being excessively bored by the concert that I had to attend when I was staying in his Palace."

Pierre Vallon laughed.

"That, of course, is an undeniable recommendation! At the same time, Your Grace, I understood that you are fond of music."

"Very fond when it is the right sort," the Duke replied. "And let me add I am looking forward to hearing what you have been composing while we have been travelling here."

"I shall be delighted to play it to you," Pierre Vallon replied, "but actually it requires a large orchestra."

"I expect the Duc will be able to supply one," the Duke answered.

"Are you so sure that your friends will welcome us?" Zoia asked. "They may think us an intolerable nuisance or maybe The Palace is full."

"Wait until you see it," the Duke replied.

They arrived the following afternoon and, as Zoia saw the tall cypress trees that had first been introduced by Catherine the Great silhouetted against a translucent sky with the blue sea beyond, she thought that she had never seen anything so lovely until she saw the Governor-General's Palace.

Then she was just spellbound by its gleaming white beauty, surrounded by flowers and shrubs that were a kaleidoscope of colour.

As they drove up to The Palace, Zoia could not help thinking that in contrast she looked dusty and travel-stained while she knew that the Duke himself was very tired. Nevertheless, when the servants fetched first one of the Governor-General's *aides-de-camp* and then His Excellency himself, there was no doubt of their welcome and Pierre Vallon need not have been concerned that he and Zoia were an embarrassment.

"I heard you conducting in London," the Governor-General said, "and I can assure you, Monsieur Vallon, that nothing could ever give me any greater pleasure than to offer you my hospitality."

When the Duke presented Zoia, the Frenchman appraised her with shrewd eyes and said,

"There is one very easy way, *mademoiselle*, into the heart of Odessa and that is beauty!"

Zoia blushed, but there was no doubt of his admiration or the way that he continued to look at her as they entered The Palace.

The Duke was too tired to do anything but fall asleep as soon as he was shown into his bedroom and helped into bed. But Zoia, after having enjoyed a warm bath, put on one of her prettiest gowns and went downstairs.

The Governor-General's wife, the Duchesse de Richelieu, made them welcome, although some of the other women staying in The Palace were not so effusive, sensing her as a rival and knowing that they could not compete with her in looks.

But the fact that they had come from Moscow and had news of the Battle of Borodino, which had only just been reported in Odessa, made Pierre Vallon the focus of attention and he had to explain in detail all that had occurred besides recounting his own interview with the Emperor Napoleon.

"How can he behave in such an uncivilised way?" the Duchesse asked. "He is nothing but a Corsican barbarian and a savage."

"I agree with you, my dear," the Governor-General said. "At the same time one has to admit that it was an amazing feat of Generalship to lead six hundred thousand men such a distance and to enter Moscow without resistance from anyone."

"I only hope he will be burnt to death with all those lovely houses!" one of the guests exclaimed. "I had intended to go to Moscow this winter for the balls.

"There will certainly be no balls," Pierre Vallon answered, "and I doubt if, by the time the French leave, there will be anything left standing except perhaps the Kremlin."

"Why should the French leave?" the Duchesse enquired.

"They will have to go," Pierre Vallon answered, "for there is not enough food to last for long except perhaps for Members of Napoleon's large Staff and what is left of the Russian population, hiding in Churches and in cellars, is already on the verge of starvation."

"It does not bear thinking about," one of the women guests cried. "I only hope that all the French, every single one of that detestable nation, will sooner or later die like rats in a trap!"

There was then an uncomfortable silence after she had spoken as the lady remembered that both the Governor-General and Pierre Vallon were French.

Then everybody started to talk hurriedly at once.

*

In the next several days Zoia suffered from no embarrassment or received anything but kindness even from the Russian guests in The Palace.

"You have Russian eyes, my dear," one old Countess said to her, "and I know that, like your grandmother and your mother, you feel things very deeply."

She gave a little sigh.

"That is to us Russians our glory and our curse. We so often touch ecstasy, but we also know despair, deep despair. You cannot have one without the other."

"I suppose not, ma'am," Zoia commented.

She knew that it was ecstasy to be with the Duke, to see him and to talk to him, but it was the darkness of despair to know that, as he grew better day by day, the time when they could be together was rapidly running out.

As soon as he had recovered from the strenuousness of the journey, he was well enough to dress and just to sit on the balcony of his large bedroom which overlooked the garden and the sea.

A few days later he was carried downstairs to sit on the verandah.

"It is so beautiful here," Zoia said again and again.

She listened to the birds in the morning and felt a touch of salt on the warm air that came from the waves moving restlessly over the sea that was vividly blue against the sunlit sky.

"There is only one thing missing," the Duke replied.

"What is that?" she asked.

"Your music."

"Do you want me to play to you?"

"I would love you to do so."

She had seen that there was a piano in the next room and, without saying anything more, she walked towards it and sat down.

The windows were all open and she could see the Duke as she played and she thought that he should listen to one of her father's compositions that described so vividly the beauty of nature.

Then, when she started playing, without really being conscious of it, she expressed in the music that her father had composed not what *he* had felt but what *she* herself was feeling.

Despite every resolution not to, her love crept into her fingers and with it the ecstasy and despair that the Countess had described so accurately.

There was the ecstasy that she had felt from the moment she had met the Duke and when his hand had first touched hers, a sensation so perfect and so beautiful that it was part of the Divine and yet a very human part of herself because she was a woman and he was a man.

She told him in her playing how she had always believed that one day she would find love as her mother had done and one day the man who had been only a dream in her heart would materialise.

Now it was real – very real – and, when she saw him, she had recognised him because already she had loved him for years or perhaps was it for centuries and in many other lives?

Then, as her love flowed from her fingers, there was the despair too and the knowledge that inevitably and inescapably they must part.

She told him how, if she never saw him again, her heart would always be with him, her prayers would always protect him and what he had evoked in her would go on living eternally because it was an indivisible part of her life.

As always when she was playing and she was carried away by the music, Zoia forgot everything except what she must express, because it swept from her like the waters of the sea.

When she finished, because it seemed as if there was nothing more to say, she was suddenly exhausted because she had poured her very self into the music that she had created.

Only then did she realise that there were a number of people listening to her including her father.

They had moved into the verandah and were sitting beside the Duke. They had made no noise, but listened in silence because it was impossible for anyone not to be moved by what they heard.

Then, as Zoia came back from the world she had been carried into by her own creation, she saw her father's face and knew that she had revealed what she felt so clearly that he was deeply touched by what he had learned but at the same time apprehensive.

With a feeling of consternation and also one of shyness that seeped deep into her soul, Zoia realised that she had betrayed herself.

Rising to her feet without an explanation or apology, she left the room, moving as if in a dream along the passages of The Palace and then up the stairs to the sanctuary of her own bedroom.

CHAPTER SEVEN

Going to her bedroom to dress for dinner Zoia the beautiful train saw lying on the bed that the Duchesse had given her.

It had been three days ago that the Governor-General had said at luncheon,

"Our most distinguished guest, the Duke of Welminster, has told me that he feels well enough to enjoy a party. I therefore intend to invite all the people to meet him, who have been longing to do so since they learnt that he had arrived in Odessa."

"A party? What sort of party?" the Duchesse enquired from the other end of the table.

The Governor-General smiled.

"Just the sort that you will enjoy, my dear, with dancing and, of course, for Monsieur Vallon's benefit, the best musicians obtainable in New Russia."

"Dancing!" the ladies exclaimed in unison and went on to add,

"What you are saying, Your Excellency, is that you are going to give a ball."

"A ball it shall be," the Governor-General promised, "and I hope our Imperial Splendour is as magnificent as His Grace enjoyed in St. Petersburg."

The Duke smiled.

"Everybody was very sober-minded in St. Petersburg. In fact, when I was staying with His Imperial Majesty, there were no balls only Receptions when everyone gossiped eternally on the same subject."

"I shall issue a decree," the Governor-General asserted, "that no one is to speak of war and we are all to be entirely frivolous and light-hearted!"

Listening, Zoia thought that it would be very exciting to be present at a grand ball such as her mother had often described to her.

She was well aware that it would be very splendid and everything would glitter from the crystal chandeliers to the bejewelled guests.

But she knew with a terrible ache in her heart that now the Duke was well, he would be planning to leave Odessa and the moment when she would see him for the last time was now approaching nearer and nearer.

The only person who did not seem to be very enthusiastic about the idea of a ball was her father, but he had always disliked formal parties and Zoia suspected that he would not be very impressed by any musicians that the Governor General would engage to entertain him.

At the same time, woman-like, she immediately began to consider what she should wear.

She wanted the Duke to admire her and it would be very humiliating to feel that she was outshone in every way by the other ladies staying in The Palace.

Fortunately among the things that she had brought with her from Moscow was one very elaborate evening gown that she had not yet worn.

And she had been keeping it for the winter balls that the Governor of Moscow, Count Rostopchin, gave in the Kremlin.

She had been invited last year, but, although she was in mourning for her mother, she had thought that it would be very exciting to accompany her father to such a function.

So she and Maria had planned together a beautiful and elaborate white gown that she hoped would gain her father's approval.

She knew, from what her mother had told her that, if the Governor-General's ball in Odessa was to rival those held in St. Petersburg, the ladies would all have trains.

This was a luxury that she did not possess and she wondered if she should explain her lack of one to her hostess and then decided against it.

She had, however, yesterday evening, been sent for by the Duchesse. When she reached the Governor-General's State apartments, she found that her hostess was lying on a couch in the window wearing an attractive *negligée*.

"Sit down, child," she ordered. "I want to talk to you. There does not seem to have been a moment since you arrived for us to have a quiet chat."

"It is very kind of you, *madame*, to have my father and myself to stay."

"Your father is my husband's concern," the Duchesse replied, "but you, because you are your mother's daughter, are mine."

"You knew my mother?" Zoia asked, her eyes lighting up.

"I met her in France just after she had married your father and before my husband and I had to flee the country unless we wished to be guillotined!"

She put out her hand to take Zoia's and added gently,

"Now she is no longer with you, I know you must miss her. You are so very like her."

Zoia's eyes filled with tears at the sympathetic note in the Duchesse's voice and, because she found it impossible to speak, the Duchesse went on,

"I know in the circumstances that you now find yourself in that your mother would wish you to enjoy the ball that is taking place tomorrow night. You must therefore allow me to give you a train to wear, which, as I expect you know, is correct on such occasions."

"I knew that, *madame*, and I was feeling embarrassed because I did not have one," Zoia responded.

"That is why I must supply your need, my dear. Look in the next room on the bed and see if you like what you see."

Zoia then went from the Duchesse's boudoir into her bedroom and saw lying on the huge carved and canopied bed, the loveliest train that she could ever have imagined.

It was of turquoise blue silk embroidered with pearls and narrowly edged with snow-white ermine.

She stared at it in delight and then went back to her hostess to say,

"It is beautiful! Really beautiful! Are you quite certain, *madame*, that you wish to give me anything so valuable? Perhaps I should just borrow it for the evening."

"It is a gift," the Duchesse said, "and I have a brooch that matches it which I would like you to wear as well."

She opened a velvet-lined box that she had beside her and Zoia saw a brooch fashioned of turquoise and diamonds in a very delicate design, which made her exclaim in delight.

She pinned it in the front of the gown she was wearing and said,

"I cannot begin to thank you for such lovely presents and I am sure that the turquoises will bring me luck, as I believe they are reputed to do."

"Here and in the Caucasus they are considered to be very lucky," the Duchesse agreed, "and perhaps that is what you are looking for at the moment."

Zoia did not answer, but the Duchesse saw the sadness in her eyes and so she then said,

"Life has been difficult for you, especially when the two nations that you belong to are at war with each other, but I have a feeling that you will find happiness when you least expect it."

"I hope – so," Zoia murmured.

Then, as she had no wish to discuss the Duke with anyone, she thanked the Duchesse again for her presents and went to her own room.

When she was alone, she asked herself how it was possible for her ever to find happiness when she must lose the Duke.

Every day he had grown stronger she had been glad both for his sake and because she felt that she had been partly instrumental in his regaining his health so quickly.

Equally she recognised that this carried her inevitably nearer to the time when they must part.

She wondered how she could bear to actually utter the word 'goodbye' and was afraid that, when the moment came, she would break down and collapse sobbing at his feet.

Then she told herself that her pride would prevent her from doing anything but behave in a dignified and proper manner.

A pride that came from the blood of the Strovolskys and their ancient heritage and the pride that was very much part of her father because he had achieved so much with his great talent.

And when she walked with the Duke in the garden and listened to him talking to her in his deep voice, she knew that her love was so overwhelming and so intense that it was hard to behave as he would expect her to do.

How, she would ask herself at times, could anyone ever call her an ice maiden when her whole body seemed to burn with hidden fires and she had an uncontrollable urge to express her love because it filled her mind, her heart and her soul to the exclusion of all else.

Ever since the day she had played to the Duke and revealed if not to him, then to her father, the depth and breadth of her feeling, she had not touched the piano.

She did not trust herself and she still felt shy and ashamed at the way that she had been carried away into proclaiming what she felt.

'It was indiscreet and foolish of me,' she berated herself.

But she felt sometimes that, if she did not express the fires that consumed her, she would explode like the gun which had injured the Duke.

Then in the quiet of the night, she would tell herself that the practical sensible French side of her nature must control the impetuous wildness of the Russian.

Yet there was not one part of her that was not desperately and massively in love.

*

The maid had prepared a bath for Zoia and it was scented with perfume that smelt to her like tuberoses, the flowers of passion.

As she lay in the warm water, it was impossible not to think of the Duke and repeat in her mind the things that he had talked about as they wandered around the garden earlier in the day.

There were other people in the house party doing the same and, although they moved out of earshot, Zoia was very conscious that they were never completely alone.

"You are really better?" she asked the Duke. "The ball tonight will not be – too much for you?"

"Maria asked me the same question," the Duke answered, "but even she has had to admit that my wounds are healed and she can no longer mollycoddle me any more than you can."

"I have no – wish to do that."

Zoia well knew, as she spoke, that it was not the truth. She wanted to keep him helpless simply so that she and Maria should be indispensable to him.

"My wounds are healed," the Duke went on, "'but I shall carry the scars as decorations, or should I say, souvenirs of the battle of Borodino for the rest of my life."

"It is something I have no wish to remember," Zoia replied. "When the servants brought you to our house in Moscow, I – thought you were – dead."

"I was not meant to die," the Duke said lightly, "and one day I shall tell you why."

She glanced at him questioningly wondering what more he would tell her, but he was not looking at her but across the garden at the sea stretching away towards the horizon.

'He is thinking of his home in England,' she thought with a little contraction of her heart and she wondered if she should ask him how soon he intended to leave Odessa.

Then she knew that she could not bear to hear the answer. It was too painful and she might even betray her true feelings when she learnt of the actual date of his departure.

"I think I shall always remember the beauty of this garden," the Duke was saying aloud, "and that you look like one of the flowers in it."

Their eyes then met and for a moment it seemed as if they were as close as they had been when he had listened to her music and known what she was thinking.

Then, before she could speak and before they could say anything further to each other, they were joined by people who wanted to talk about the ball.

After her bath Zoia sat in front of the mirror while her maid arranged her hair in the more fashionable style that she had worn in Moscow.

Among her mother's jewellery that she had brought away with her was a lovely wreath of diamonds that Natasha Strovolsky had been given on her seventeenth birthday.

Reverently Zoia had taken it from its wrappings and felt that, if she wore it tonight, her mother would be thinking of her at the first grand ball that she had ever attended.

Zoia had seen her mother wearing the wreath on occasions when she had accompanied her father to some guished function that she was too young to be invited

"You look like the Fairy Princess, Mama," she had said once, "and Papa is, of course. Prince Charming."

"That is what he has always been to me," her mother replied.

She put up her hand and touched the wreath on her head and then said with a smile,

"I am so glad I can hold my own with all the important and distinguished people who will be there tonight. I so very nearly sold this when we first married and were very poor before your father was recognised as a great musician, but he insisted on my keeping it and now I am glad I did."

It was not because it was valuable, Zoia knew, but because it stood for everything that her mother had given up for love.

'This was Mama's Imperial Splendour,' she thought. 'Tonight it will be mine and maybe I shall never go to a ball like this again.'

She was certain that, when they reached France with the War still raging, there would be few festive occasions at which people would be dressed as they would be tonight.

With the wreath on her head she certainly looked very regal and the maid helped her first into her gown and then fixed the exquisite turquoise blue train to her shoulders.

It gave her a presence and a dignity that she had never had before, but all she wondered, as she looked at her reflection in the mirror, was what the Duke would think of her.

The door opened and her father came into the room.

"You are ready, Papa?" Zoia asked him.

She turned from the mirror so that he could look at h.

"I want to speak to you," Pierre Vallon stated.

Her expression changed. She made a gesture to the maid to leave the room and waited until the door had closed behind her.

"What is it, Papa?"

He walked towards her and she knew instinctively that he was feeling for his words.

"What – is it?" she asked again.

"There is a Turkish ship in the Port of Odessa," Pierre Vallon replied. "It will leave on the dawn tide."

Zoia drew in her breath.

"I have spoken to the Captain," her father went on, "and he will take us to Marseilles. It is an opportunity that we cannot afford to miss."

"But, Papa – " Zoia began.

He interrupted her.

"Before you say anything, let me tell you that a British Man-of-War is expected in two or three days' time. I overheard the Duke telling one of His Excellency's *aides-de-camp* that he intended to ask for passage on it to England."

Zoia was very still.

Then she sat down on the stool that she had just vacated, feeling that her legs would no longer carry her.

"What I want you to do," Pierre Vallon said, "is to leave the ball and drive straight to the ship where I will be waiting for you."

"Leave the – ball?" Zoia repeated stupidly.

"It would be wisest, my dear. What is the point of torturing yourself by saying 'goodbye' to the Duke, knowing that there will be nothing to gain from it but added unhappiness to what you are feeling already?"

"You know – how much I – love him, Papa."

"Yes, I know, but as you agreed from the very beginning, there can be no happy ending to your story. Therefore I think my method of leaving is kinder for you and kinder for him as well."

"Kinder for – him?" Zoia questioned.

"What can he do, but thank you? The Duke of Welminster is as important in England as your grandfather was in Russia. They both had a pride in their family and their blood that would not allow them to lower their standards of behaviour for anything. Not even love!"

Zoia clenched her fingers together until the knuckles showed white.

She knew that what her father was saying to her was true, but that made it no less hurtful and no less an instrument of despair.

"You have to be brave, dearest," Pierre Vallon cautioned, "and quite frankly this will be the easiest way."

He did not wait for her answer but went on,

"I have spoken to Maria. She is already packing. She and Jacques will leave The Palace late in the evening and drive to the ship."

Zoia waited, knowing that what she was to hear she should do was, as it were, the fall of the axe.

"I will be waiting at the end of the garden for you in a closed carriage," Pierre Vallon went on. "It might evoke awkward questions if we leave the ballroom together."

Perhaps the Duke would stop us, Zoia pondered.

But she knew that there was no point in saying such a thing aloud and she merely went on listening as her father continued,

"I understand that the Governor-General has arranged for a gypsy orchestra to play at about midnight and for their women to dance. I am sorry we shall miss it, but I suggest that, as soon as everybody's attention is concentrated on them, you slip away through the garden to where I shall be waiting for you."

"It – seems very – rude," Zoia murmured because she felt that something was expected of her.

"I have already thought of that," Pierre Vallon replied. "I have written a letter both to the Governor-General and to the Duchesse thanking them for their hospitality."

"And the – Duke?"

Zoia could not help the question that seemed to burst from her lips.

"When the Duke learns that we have gone," Pierre Vallon replied, "he will appreciate our tact and the way we have saved him from being involved in something that might prove uncomfortably emotional."

There was a cynical twist to his lips as he added,

"The English dislike anything that might break down their traditional reserve."

"You really don't think he will – consider it – unkind and – remiss of us not to tell him what we are – doing?" Zoia asked.

"Do you want me to be frank with you?" Pierre Vallon enquired.

"Of course, Papa."

"Then if I am honest, I know that the Duke finds you very beautiful and very desirable, but we have to face the truth, dearest, and know that he wants more than that in the woman he will make his wife."

Zoia closed her eyes as if to protect herself from a blow.

Then she said in a voice that sounded dull with misery even to herself,

"I will do what you – want me to do – Papa – because I trust you – and perhaps it is right that we should save the Duke – any embarrassment."

"You are very sensible, my dearest," Pierre Vallon said, "and believe me, if I could save you from what you are suffering and if I could add your despair to my own and leave you free, I would do so."

His words brought Zoia to her feet.

She moved into his arms and put her cheek against his.

"I thought – love meant happiness – and joy," she sighed, "but what I am – feeling is a – darkness where I am sure that the sun will – never shine again."

"That is how I felt when your mother died, but life goes on and perhaps one day you will find somebody else you can love and be happy with him."

Zoia wanted to cry out that it would never happen, but because she did not wish to upset her father, she said nothing and she found a little comfort from his arms.

They stood entwined for a long moment until Pierre Vallon said in a practical tone,

"We must not be late for dinner. His Excellency is making this a very special evening for us as well as for the Duke, which, of course, I do appreciate."

He went from the room and Zoia returned to the dressing table to stand looking at her reflection in the mirror.

She was only surprised that her appearance did not seem to have changed.

She had a feeling that her father had taken away her youth and she would not have been astonished to see herself old, wrinkled and grey-haired.

Instead she looked very lovely, except that, deep in the purple depths of her eyes, there was an inexpressible pain.

*

The ballroom with its huge chandeliers, each holding hundreds of tapers, was fragrant with flowers and on the carved and gilt cornice which encircled the room, there were lines of lit candles, an idea that Zoia had never seen before.

If the setting was magnificent, so were the guests.

Never had she imagined that women could wear quite so many glittering jewels from the magnificent tiaras on their heads to the buckles on their shoes.

The Duchesse and her Ladies-in-Waiting were wearing the Russian Court dress of white silk, cut low with a close-fitting bodice and a red train that was gold-embroidered.

They also wore the Ribbon of the Order of St. Catherine with its diamond cross.

And the men were determined not to be outdone, for everyone present was either in a spectacular and splendid uniform and was covered with decorations with ribbons across their chests.

The Duke wore the Order of the Garter below the knee of his left leg.

There were Huzzar Officers in white and gold, Court Chamberlains in blue frockcoats, stiff with gold, and young Circassians in high black or white sheepskin hats.

The evening was a Fairytale spectacle, Zoia knew, from the moment she had entered the huge dining room to see a breath-taking display of gold plate on the table and to find to her astonishment that she was seated on the right of the Governor-General.

The Duke was seated on the right of the Duchesse with Pierre Vallon on her left and the Governor-General explained to everyone that she and her father, like the Duke, were the Guests of Honour of the evening.

"Everybody here has come to meet you," he informed Zoia with a smile.

"Despite the fact that we are – French?" Zoia asked in a low voice.

"As I am," the Governor-General replied. "My dear, music is an international language that knows no boundaries and no barriers and your father, in my estimation, is King of a far greater Empire than anything that Napoleon Bonaparte might be trying to achieve."

Her father was certainly enjoying himself, Zoia thought, and she felt that for her too it would have been the most wonderful evening she had ever known, except that it was the end of the chapter that she had spoken to the Duke about as they had left Moscow.

'A very short – chapter,' she ruminated wistfully.

She could not help feeling that those that came after would be pale and uninspiring and she shrank from thinking of what it would mean when she would never see the Duke again.

'I shall be alone, as I have never been alone before.' she thought, 'and loneliness without love will be colder than any Siberian winter!'

The Duke was looking so magnificent that she found it difficult to see anyone else in the glittering company and, when they entered the ballroom, he came to her side to say,

"I really cannot ask you to dance with me, Zoia, for I have been forbidden by Maria to do anything so adventurous. But will you sit and talk to me?"

"You know I would like to do so," she answered.

She thought she would go with him there and then, but the Governor-General asked her to dance with him and it was impossible to refuse what was in effect a Royal Command.

When that dance was over, there were other inescapable partners and it was over an hour before eventually the Duke came to her side and, without saying anything, they moved away together through the wide open windows of the ballroom onto the terrace outside.

It was a night of stars with a crescent moon moving up the sky and the garden, with soft lights concealed amongst the flowers, was a poem of beauty. Beyond there was the mystery of the sea.

As they sat down on a seat in the shadows, they could hear the music in the ballroom behind them and for a moment Zoia could find nothing to say until the Duke asked her,

"You are worried?"

"How do you – know I am?"

"I thought we had agreed long ago that I can read your thoughts."

Zoia did not reply because she was hoping that at this particular moment he could do no such thing. She felt something like panic sweep over her only to reassure herself that she was being needlessly afraid.

It was one thing for him to understand what she played on the piano, but quite another to be aware that within an hour or so they would never see each other again.

"Are you going to tell me what is troubling you or must I guess?" the Duke quizzed her.

"Why – should I be troubled by – anything?" she replied. "It is a – wonderful evening and a great – tribute to you."

"And, of course, to you as well," he replied. "Do I have to tell you how lovely you look tonight?"

There was a note in his voice that made her vibrate to him.

Then she told herself that he was just being polite and she forced herself to say,

"Everybody has been just – so kind – Her Excellency gave me this beautiful train – and I shall always remember this moment – here in Odessa."

"There are other moments for us to remember," the Duke ventured.

"Will you – remember – them?" Zoia enquired.

She could not help the question because she wanted so much to hear his answer.

"I think what I will remember most vividly is when I came back to consciousness after I had been wounded and saw your face looking down at me."

Zoia felt herself quiver. She had longed for him to talk to her like this and yet there had never seemed to be an opportunity until now.

"I have a feeling," the Duke then went on, "that you were calling me back through the darkness that encompassed me. I knew, when I had thought deeply about it, that even in my unconsciousness I had been conscious of you."

That was what she had wanted him to feel when she had called him desperately back to life from the darkness of death.

"Do you really think that is an event that I could ever forget?" the Duke asked.

"Please – remember me – always."

The words were spoken impulsively and there was a pleading expression in her face as she looked up at the Duke.

His eyes met hers and it seemed that he was looking straight into her heart and they were both very still.

Then, as if it came from another world, a voice said,

"So here you are, Mademoiselle Vallon, I have been looking for you. His Excellency wishes you to dance the mazurka with him."

For a moment Zoia found it hard to understand what was being said to her.

Then, as if she jerked herself black to reality, she rose to her feet.

"It is – very kind of His Excellency," she managed to say to the *aide-de-camp* who had been sent in search of her.

"Let me escort you to the ballroom, *mademoiselle*."

"Thank – you," Zoia replied.

She could not look at the Duke.

She felt only as if she was being dragged away from him.

She wanted so much to hold onto him and beg him not to let her go.

Instead she followed the *aide-de-camp* back into the ballroom, thanked the Governor-General for his kindness and they started the mazurka together in an animated manner.

After that it seemed impossible to escape from the men who surrounded her.

Every time a dance ended she looked around her frantically for the Duke, but before she could see him or move towards him through the crowds, somebody else had already claimed her and she was forced to dance with them.

She danced automatically and had no idea what her partners said to her or what she said to them.

She was only conscious that time was going faster and faster and that all she wanted was to spend the last minutes of it with the man she loved so much.

Then, despairingly, she realised that there was no sign of her father either and she knew only too well where he had gone.

The dance came to an end. Now there was a roll of drums and on the steps into the ballroom there appeared a gypsy orchestra resplendent in their colourful clothes.

Their black eyes echoed their black hair and their high cheekbones singled them out as people of another race and, as Zoia was aware, another culture.

The guests were all moving away from the centre of the floor, the older women seating themselves on the chairs and sofas around the room, the gentlemen standing beside them or in groups waiting to applaud the entertainment that their host had provided for them.

Then, as the gypsy women with their full skirts, gold necklaces and jingling bracelets danced onto the floor with bare feet, Zoia knew that this was the moment when she had to leave.

She looked around once more hoping to see the Duke and yet fully knowing, if she did so, that there was nothing she could do about it.

It was too late now for them to talk and besides what was there to say except that she loved him with all her heart and soul?

It was easy, while everybody's attention was fixed on the gypsies, for her to slip through one of the open windows onto the terrace where there were white marble steps going down into the garden.

There was nobody to notice her moving down them and she crossed the smooth green lawn between the beds of flowers until she saw another flight of steps.

As she reached them, she looked down and saw a carriage, as she had expected.

It was closed and there were two men on the box, one of whom jumped down as soon as she appeared and went to the carriage door.

Feeling as if she walked to her doom, Zoia descended the steps slowly.

The door of the carriage was open and, moving into the darkness inside, she sat down on the back seat, aware as she did so that her father was there waiting for her in the darkness.

The carriage door was shut, the footman climbed up onto the box and the horses started off.

Zoia bent forward to take one last look through the window at the garden that she had just left.

'Goodbye – my love – my only love – now and for Eternity,' she breathed in her heart.

Then, as she leaned back in the seat fighting the tears that blinded her eyes, a deep voice asked,

"Who are you saying 'goodbye' to, Zoia?"

She gave a cry both of shock and astonishment, for it was not her father who spoke but the Duke!

She turned her face towards him and in the light of the lamps on the drive that they were travelling down, she could see his face and his eyes gazing into hers.

For a moment she was incapable of speech and then almost incoherently she asked him,

"Why – are you – here? What – has happened?"

"That is really the question that I should be asking you," the Duke replied. "How could you imagine that you could leave me and I not be aware of it?"

"B-but – Papa said – "

"Your father is now on board the Turkish ship that will carry him to France," the Duke interrupted. "I have only the one question to ask of you, Zoia, and I wish you to answer me truthfully."

"What is – it?" she whispered.

"It is quite simple," the Duke answered. "I want you to tell me who you love best, your father or me."

For a moment she thought that she could not have heard him aright.

Then, as she looked up at him, she had a fleeting glimpse of an expression on his face that she had not seen before and instantly felt her heart turn over in her breast.

"It is a very important question," the Duke insisted, "because the choice is yours. I can take you now to your father so that you can leave with him or you can stay with me."

It was impossible for Zoia to speak and he went on,

"It is just a question of *love*, that is the answer I want you to give me."

"I – love you!" Zoia whispered. "I love you – desperately – *but* – "

The Duke's arms went around her as he interrupted her.

"There are no 'buts'," he insisted. "If you love me, if you really love me, that is all I want to know."

"I love – you!" Zoia answered him at once.

The words seemed to come from her very soul.

The Duke's arms tightened around her and, as she lifted her face to him, his lips came down on hers.

For a moment she was so bewildered by what had happened that she could feel nothing save amazement and then the pressure of the Duke's mouth evoked the ecstasy that she had always felt when they were close to each other, but now far more intense and more perfect so that she wished she might die as nothing could ever be so Divine or so utterly and completely perfect.

His arms held her closer and his kiss became more demanding and more insistent and she felt as if the fire that had burnt within her rose until it reached her lips and both she and the Duke were lost in the burning wonder of it.

How long the kiss lasted she had no idea. She only knew that, when the Duke raised his head, words like music came from her in a paean of wonder.

"I love you – I – love – you!"

"And I love you!" the Duke insisted. "I have loved you, my darling, ever since I first saw you. But I wanted to be well before I could tell you the depth and splendour of my love."

"Can this be – true?" she asked. "Do you really – love me? I cannot believe it."

"I love you! Now that you have made your choice, my darling, we are going straight away to be married."

"To be – *married*?" Zoia stammered.

"It will make everything so much easier, my darling, when we set off for England and I should tell you that I have already had your father's blessing."

"Papa – knows you intended to – do this?"

"When I knew that you were leaving me, I was determined not to let you go."

"How – did you – know I was – leaving?"

"You told me."

"I – told you?"

He smiled as his lips sought hers again.

For a moment neither of them could speak.

Then he said,

"It would be very difficult, my precious, for you ever to deceive me. I knew when I watched you at dinner what you were thinking and, when we sat together on the terrace, I was sure of what had been planned."

"How – could you have – known that?" Zoia asked.

"Can you, of all people, ask that question?" he enquired.

She gave a little laugh remembering how he had read her thoughts when she had first played to him.

"I then realised," the Duke went on, "that I had been somewhat remiss in not having taken action before. I found your father and told him what I wanted and he agreed that, as far as he was concerned, it was a perfect solution to everything that was worrying him."

"And Papa still – wishes to go to – France?" Zoia asked.

"He thought that it was an opportunity not to be missed. Finding a neutral ship is not easy," the Duke replied, "and I think too he is being tactful, knowing that we would want to be alone together."

There was just a touch of anxiety in his voice as he asked,

"You do want to be alone with me, my darling?"

He knew her answer before the words came to her lips and once again he was kissing her and, Zoia felt, drawing her very heart from her body and making it his.

The carriage came to a standstill.

"Everything has been arranged for us by one of His Excellency's able *aides-de-camp*," the Duke said, "I thought, my precious, that you would like to be married in the faith that your mother belonged to. And it seemed most appropriate when we are here in Russia."

"You – know it would – make me so happy," Zoia murmured in a low voice.

The door of the carriage was opened and she saw that they stood outside a small Church. It was built in the old Russian style and painted with bright colours and with gold cupolas rising one above another.

The Duke took her hand and she was glad that she had a train to trail behind her as they walked into the Church.

There was the scent of incense and there were hundreds of glittering lights before the sacred icons that hung on every wall and every pillar.

A Priest was waiting for them with two servers holding Imperial Crowns, which would be raised over their heads as they were married.

Zoia slipped her hand into the Duke's.

They were so closely attuned that she knew that for him the Service would be as sacred and binding as it was for her.

She was sure that her mother was close to her and inexpressibly happy that her daughter, like herself, had found the man she really loved.

'Thank you, thank you God,' Zoia prayed in her heart. 'You have given me the man I adore. Help me to make him happy and – show me how to keep his love for ever and ever.'

*

Driving away from the Church, Zoia felt as if she was in a dream and it could not really be true that she had passed through such a mystical and spiritual experience and still be in the ordinary mundane world.

The Duke's arms were both round her and his lips seeking hers added to the illusion that nothing was real except for him and their love.

He kissed her until she felt as if they were no longer human but Divine and even closer still to God than they had been during the beautiful Wedding Service.

"My own perfect, lovely little wife," he murmured.

"Say that – again," she pleaded. "I was so certain – so convinced – that you could never marry me – that I cannot believe I am really your – wife."

"I will make you very sure of it in a little while," the Duke replied.

"You will – never – regret having – married me?"

"Only if you cease to love me."

"I shall love you completely every hour I live and with every breath I breathe," Zoia said passionately.

"My precious!"

The Duke's lips were on hers and she felt the passion draw a response from hers.

He kissed her until she felt breathless and her heart was beating wildly in her breast.

As the horses slowed down and the carriage came to a standstill, Zoia felt regretfully that they must come back to earth.

She felt that the Governor-General and the Duchesse would be waiting to congratulate them on being married, but she shrank from the thought of anyone at this moment breaking in on the intimacy and the closeness that she felt in the Duke's arms.

Then, as the door of the carriage was opened, she realised that they were not outside The Palace but a much smaller building also built of white stone.

She was suddenly aware that it was one of the small Pavilions that she knew were built in the grounds of the

Governor-General's Palace and she had been told that they were usually occupied by distinguished guests who brought their own retinue of servants with them.

The Duke once again knew what she was thinking and he told her,

"We shall be alone, my darling. I want it as much if not more than you do."

He drew her inside the Pavilion and then closed the door behind them and she heard the carriage draw away.

Now there were flowers that scented the air and there were shaded lights to reveal that the place was furnished with many treasures, but there appeared to be no one in the Pavilion but themselves.

The Duke took her through a sitting room and then beyond to a room lit only by a few candles and there was a magnificent bed hung with turquoise blue silk from a gilt corolla of carved angels.

The ceiling was painted with Gods, Goddesses and cupids and on one wall there was a huge window with its curtains drawn back so that Zoia could see the stars.

With his arms around her the Duke took her across the room to the bed and she realised that below them there was the sea reflecting the light of the pale moon so that it shimmered silver on the surface of the water.

"This – cannot really be – happening," she whispered in a low voice.

"It *is* happening, my darling one," he replied, "and now at last you are mine! Not just for tonight but for all the years ahead and beyond them for Eternity."

He pulled her close to him and went on,

"I seriously believe that I have been searching for you through centuries of time and now I have found you, I will never lose you again."

"How – could you – say anything so – wonderful to me?" she asked. "It is – what I too believe in my heart – but I thought I had to – go away."

"How could you imagine that anything could matter except for our love?" he asked. "How could you think for even one moment that anything else was of any consequence in the whole wide world?"

Zoia gave a little sigh and put her cheek against his shoulder.

"I thought that you were part of the Imperial Splendour that I had seen in St. Petersburg," she said, "that condemned my mother when she ran away from it."

"The only splendour that matters to us is the splendour of love, of our love, darling and I want you to tell me that you believe it is the truth."

"I have – always believed it," Zoia said, "but I thought, because you were so – important, because in the eyes of the Russians, Papa was presumptuous to marry my Mama, you would never think me – good enough to be your – wife."

"You are not only my wife but a spiritual ideal I shall worship for the rest of my life," the Duke vowed.

"Suppose – I fail you – ?"

"I would stake the life you have given me that it will never happen."

The note of sincerity in his voice made Zoia give a little cry and lift her face to his.

She thought that he would kiss her. Instead he looked down for a long moment into her eyes and she knew that he was searching deep into her heart and finding what he had always sought.

He drew her away from the window and very gently took the diamond wreath from her hair and undid the train from her shoulders.

As it fell to the ground, she trembled and felt shy as she could feel his hands undoing her gown.

Then his lips held her captive again.

The flames that Zoia felt deep within her rose higher and higher as he kissed her eyes, her lips, the softness of her neck and her breasts.

She knew that the Duke was right and that there was no splendour to equal their love.

What they felt for each other was a part of the stars in the sky, which glittered more dazzlingly than any jewels and deeper than the sea that moved beneath them.

The pomp and circumstance and the social distinctions that meant so much to those of Imperial rank were of no value or consequence.

"I love – you – "

The words seemed to vibrate between them and the Duke answered,

"I love your beauty, my glorious wife, and adore your mind, but I worship your spirit and your soul, which speaks to me in your music.

"I – told you – of my love?"

"I understood exactly what you were feeling, but tell me now that you love me and want me as I want you."

"I – want – you – I want you desperately and – wildly with all – of me."

"My precious, my adorable, mystical little wife!"

Zoia could feel the Duke's heart beating frantically against hers as he picked her up in his arms and laid her on the bed.

A moment later he was beside her, his lips seeking hers and his hands touching her body.

Then there was only him and the fires that burned within them burst into a conflagration.

The splendour of love covered them like the moonlight on the sea and the ecstasy in their hearts carried them towards the stars, higher and higher until they became one and indivisible with God and the Divine.

OTHER BOOKS IN THIS SERIES

The Barbara Cartland Eternal Collection is the unique opportunity to collect all five hundred of the timeless beautiful romantic novels written by the world's most celebrated and enduring romantic author.

Named the Eternal Collection because Barbara's inspiring stories of pure love, just the same as love itself, the books will be published on the internet at the rate of four titles per month until all five hundred are available.

The Eternal Collection, classic pure romance available worldwide for all time.